Idioms & Short Stories

Also by David Hastings

Over the Mountains of the Sea
Extra! Extra! How the people made the news
The Many Deaths of Mary Dobie
Odyssey of the Unknown Anzac
The Vocabulary Detective: How to get meaning from context
Look Back: how to talk about the past in English

Visit David Hastings' author page at Amazon.com
https://www.amazon.com/author/davidhastings01

David Hastings at Goodreads
https://www.goodreads.com/davidhastings01

Idioms & Short Stories

The keys to natural English
B1-C1

David Hastings

DMH Press

First published 2024
DMH Press
Auckland
New Zealand

© 2024 David Hastings
All rights reserved

ISBN: 9798320828299

This book is copyright. Apart from fair dealing for the purpose of private study, research, criticism or review, no part may be reproduced for any purpose without prior permission of the publisher. The moral rights of the author have been asserted.

Cover design: Micaela Hastings
www.mhastingsdesign.com

Cover image: Shutterstock

Table of Contents

Introduction 1

Scary night of lights 7

The first time 15

A bird in the hand 29

Life's lessons 41

A piece of advice 55

Taken for a fool 69

A date to remember 87

The one true thing 99

Glossary 107

Answers 145

Bibliography 147

Introduction

One of the biggest problems and disappointments that many language students encounter is that, despite spending a lot of time on grammar and vocabulary, they find they still don't understand what is being said out on the streets, in bars, at parties and at work. An advanced student once told me this problem was especially bad when native speakers were talking among themselves. His experience was echoed by his classmates, all of whom said it was almost as though native speakers were communicating in a language or dialect that was different to the one in the textbooks.

Although this is not strictly true, the students did have a point. Casual speech is inventive, ever-changing, and littered with slang, colloquialisms and expressions that go in and out of fashion and which often diverge dramatically from formal, grammatically correct speech. In other words, it is idiomatic, and idioms often defy logic and the rules of grammar and vocabulary.

For instance, what do you think when someone says, "I'm **all ears**"? Or talks about **a bird in the hand** or **coming a**

Introduction

cropper? And if your friend tells you the work was **meat and drink**, would you imagine that they were referring to what they had for dinner last night? And if they said there was "**no skin off my nose**", would they mean that they had had an accident but, luckily, escaped without injury? If you were tempted to answer yes to the last two questions, you would be wrong. They were both examples of expressions that have nothing whatsoever to do with the literal meaning of the words they contain.

One of the most important challenges as you move from intermediate to advanced levels, is to **come to grips with** idioms like these so that you won't feel lost listening to people in the real world, outside the classroom. And, just as important, so that you can sound more natural when speaking yourself.

This book aims to help you overcome that challenge. It consists of eight short stories, all of which are light and amusing and have twists in the tail, or unexpected endings. The first thing to do is read the stories and enjoy them without worrying too much about the bits you don't understand. Next, look at the highlighted phrases which are all idioms, including expressions, proverbs and phrasal verbs.

Before doing anything else, you should try to work out the meaning of these idioms from the context. **In a nutshell**, you do this by searching the surrounding text for clues such as synonyms, definitions, examples, comparisons and contrasts. There is a good example of this in the preceding paragraph where the idiom "twists in the tail" is immediately followed by a synonymous phrase "unexpected endings".

Idioms & Short Stories

You can find out more detail in the first book of this series, *The Vocabulary Detective: How to get meaning from context* (available on Amazon). A good idea is to keep a lookout for signpost words in the text that tell you where the clues are.

For instance, the phrase "in other words" tells you that what you have just read or heard is going to be repeated in a slightly different way. The phrases "on the contrary" or "in contrast to" tell you that you are going to see or hear something that is different from or opposite to what you have just read. These details are useful in helping you work out the meaning of unknown words and phrases.

Once you have tried to work out the meaning, check your understanding by doing the exercises at the end of each story which consist of numbered sentences with gaps in them and a selection of idioms. Your task is to match the idioms with the gaps in the sentences. As with the stories, there are clues to the meaning of the idiom in most of the sentences.

For example, in the First Steps exercise at the end of 'A date to remember' on page 94, sentence (2) reads: "I was … as she told me about what happened at the office Christmas party when a couple of our colleagues got drunk and tried to throw the CEO in the river".

Your task is to select the missing idiom from a list that includes **go out on a date**, **get the impression**, **nothing of the kind** and **all ears**. The answer is **all ears**. All the answers are on pages 145-46.

Having read the stories, worked out the meaning from context and done the exercises, you will be ready to look up the idioms in the glossary at the end of the book. This gives

Introduction

guidance on how to use the idioms in these stories and points to some related expressions, and variations. It also has tips to help you remember them through the etymology – that is the origins of the expressions – and by pointing to some popular songs which use idioms in their chorus lines and therefore are very useful in helping you to recall them.

For instance, the expression **fool's game** is illustrated in the chorus of Bonnie Tyler's hit *It's a Heartache*. Listen to that a few times and you will never forget the expression and what it means.

The glossary is not meant to be, by any means, a comprehensive dictionary of all the idioms in the English language. That would require an enormous book which would be out of date as soon as it was printed, given that idiomatic language changes so fast.

Rather, the idea is to give you a feel for idioms so that you notice them and can incorporate them into your vocabulary as necessary. After all, this is what native speakers of English do all the time when new idioms suddenly appear and, no doubt, it is what you do in your first language too.

For an example of how this works, look at 'The First Time', pages 17-18, in which the narrator works out from the context the meaning of unfamiliar word used by a deer hunter.

The idioms in this book fall into two broad categories:

Collocations: These are words that naturally fit together. For instance, **frayed nerves**, **fruitless day**, **high hopes**, **milling around**, **night out**. I include phrasal verbs and multi word verbs in this category: **pick me up**, **size up**, **warn off**, **catch up** and so on.

Idioms & Short Stories

Expressions and sayings: These can be proverbs or fixed ways of expressing particular ideas **come to grips with, a bird in the hand, meat and drink, no skin off my nose**.

Note that the phrases and expressions that appear in bold type throughout the book are referenced in the glossary.

This is the third volume in the Vocabulary Detective series. The first, *The Vocabulary Detective*, encourages you to develop the skill of working out the meaning of unknown words and phrases from the context. The second, *Look Back*, is about the many different ways of talking about the past in English, stressing meaning before grammar. *Idioms & Short Stories* deals with the keys to understanding and speaking more natural, informal English.

Like the first two volumes, this one is not enough by itself. Rather, you should think of it as the first of a series of stepping stones on the way to mastering idiomatic English. The first steps being to recognise the idiom, understand it and practise it using the exercises in this book. But to truly master it, you should put the book down and step out into the real world and have real conversations with real people.

Scary night of lights

On the day the Martians came to town, I was a police reporter working on the early-morning shift for a radio station. I started at 5am and I worked out of a small dingy office that opened on to the street just a few metres from the main entrance to the police headquarters, an old-fashioned skyscraper built from brick in the art deco style with a tall radio mast on the rooftop pointing up into the sky. It was a great spot to watch the city wake up and to keep an eye all the **comings and goings** of the police officers, **night and day**.

The aim of the job was to gather all the news and information I could get about whatever had happened on the mean streets of the city during the night and write reports for the morning bulletins to keep the good citizens informed as they had their breakfast and made their way to work. I covered anything that was out of the ordinary, anything that disrupted the normal, expected routines of life. That meant everything from murders and robberies to traffic accidents and fires if they were serious enough.

Scary night of lights

But until that morning, I had never covered a visit by **extra-terrestrial** beings to our planet.

The day had started as it always did, with a taxi coming to **pick me up** about fifteen minutes before I was due to start work. It was still dark and there was no public transport operating, so the radio station paid for taxis to make sure all the staff got to work on time.

Before arriving at my house, the taxi had picked up the producer of the early-morning bulletins as usual. His name was Eric, and he was always smoking, even at that time of the morning. He never said anything to me, not even "good morning".

The fact was that Eric had a hangover most of the time and never liked to speak to anyone until after the midday bulletins had gone to air and even then, he didn't say much. Although, as a journalist, he was a man of words in his profession, he was a man of very few words in his social life, **such as it was**. Mostly, he just went to the pub after work. He got drunk in the afternoons and eventually went home to sleep until the early hours, when he would get up and repeat the process.

On this particular day, we went to work in silence as usual, but when the taxi **dropped me off** at the police station, there was an unusually large number of people there for that time of the morning. They were **milling around** outside the main entrance and were in a highly excited state. Something big must have happened I thought.

Was it a murder? A fire? Or some disaster that was causing so many people to be rushing around in a state of panic at five o'clock in the morning?

I asked the duty sergeant on the front desk of the police station, and he told me that throughout the night, two UFOs, unidentified flying objects, had been buzzing the city.

Flying saucers! Here, in our city! This was a very big story; you did not need to be a great reporter to see that.

Many people had been out in the streets and had seen them in the form of two brilliant lights. They had buzzed cars and taxis and even a police patrol car.

The officers in the police car were so frightened that they switched on their flashing lights and sirens in the hope of scaring the UFOs away. But it didn't work. The UFOs were not scared away, on the contrary, they continued following the patrol car whichever way it turned.

If it turned to the left, the two UFOs also turned left. And if it went right, the UFOs did the same.

Other people told of the same experience. It seemed like these UFOs could be everywhere at once and no one could get away from them. One man fled straight to police headquarters where he arrived shaking and panic stricken.

Still others were ringing radio stations to describe what had happened to them and what they had seen. The stories were always the same, two brilliant lights that appeared to be following everyone wherever they went.

It seemed supernatural or, at least, **extra-terrestrial**. It seemed like the Martians had finally arrived!

The sergeant told me he had been to the roof of the police headquarters to see for himself. What he saw when he stood next to the great radio aerial, confirmed the testimony of all the other witnesses. Two bright lights in the dark sky, only now

Scary night of lights

they were not moving. They were just hovering over the city as though they had paused their pursuit for a moment.

All of this was **meat and drink** for a news reporter. A fantastic story that would be of interest to just about everyone and there were many people who wanted to tell their stories about what they had seen and experienced. And so I did many interviews and in the next few hours filed rolling updates of the story about the mystery lights over the city.

It was by far the biggest story that morning and journalists were saying that it would make headlines right around the world. I was feeling pretty pleased with myself because, on account of my early start, I had been first with the news.

It had been a frantic few hours and now it was breakfast time and I was just contemplating going to have something to eat when the phone rang. It was Eric, the editor of very few words. He was speaking to me for the first time that day. I foolishly thought for a moment that he was going to congratulate me on a job well done. But no.

"Have you contacted an astronomer?" he said. His commanding tone suggested it was less a question and more an order.

"No, why?" I replied, failing to pick up on his real intent.

"Because," he said in a sarcastic, patronising voice, "it is not possible that those lights were Martians. But what is certain is that an astronomer will know the truth."

So, I rang the observatory and spoke to an astronomer who, with his colleagues, was **splitting his sides laughing** over the news reports and the widespread fear that the lights were UFOs.

"No way," he said. "Not a chance in the world."

He explained that the lights were the planets Mars and Venus in a very rare position. They were much lower on the horizon than normal and appeared to be much closer to each other than they usually were.

The effect was that they looked much bigger and shone with a light much brighter than normal. And, if you were in a moving vehicle, they would create an optical illusion that they were following you wherever you went. Conversely, if you stood still, they would appear to stop too.

So, there it was. The **unvarnished truth** had nothing to do with flying saucers or little green men from Mars and everything to do with the position of the planets and the properties of light.

So, I wrote another story to resolve the mystery and, again, I was ahead of the pack.

For instance, the afternoon newspaper did not make the call to the observatory and the main headline on their front page that day said, "Scary Night of Lights". Their report made no mention of the planets or optical illusions but there was a lot of speculation about UFOs.

On the morning that these things happened, I had not noticed the lights myself as we were coming to work. But the next day I looked out for them, and I must say I was very surprised at how big and bright they were. Not as big and bright as a full moon, obviously, but they looked like a couple of car headlights on full beam up in the sky.

And yes, they appeared to be following us. It felt strange, even though by now I knew it was all an optical illusion.

Scary night of lights

As I watched them, I said to Eric, "just look at those lights. They're fantastic, it's no wonder that so many people were **scared out of their wits** when they didn't know what they really were".

But Eric did not look. Nor did he say anything. He just continued puffing on his cigarette and we travelled on in silence, as always.

First steps

Fill in the gaps in sentences (1)-(11) with the appropriate idioms from the list below.

(1) The team arrived at the airport late at night and were disappointed to find that there was no one waiting to … and take them to their hotel. Instead, they caught a taxi which dropped them off at their hotel in the early hours of the morning.

(2) When we were kids, we lived on the side of a hill overlooking a harbour and there was nothing better than spending a lazy summer's afternoon just watching the … of all the ships, from container vessels and cruise ships to trawlers and pleasure craft.

(3) Most people would find it daunting to have to organise our town's annual arts festival, but it was … to her.

(4) When the agent told them that the house they had just rented was haunted, they took it as a joke. What fun to spend the weekend in a haunted house. But on Saturday night, when the wind was howling outside, they heard heavy footfalls in the passageway and, when someone or something turned the doorknob and the door slowly creaked open, they were ….

(5) The government said they were the only ones able to give the ..., but no one believed them.

(6) The summer is over, ... It never seemed to stop raining and was quite cold.

(7) When our friends were going home after the holidays, I picked them up at their hotel and ... at the airport in plenty of time to catch their flight to London.

(8) It was one of the funniest things I've ever seen. I just about ....

(9) The deadline was looming and there was so much to do that we worked ... for a week to get the job done.

(10) We have names for those who come from other planets. To some they are ..., to others, Martians, and to others still, just little green men. But whatever you call them, one thing is certain: no one has ever seen one.

(11) I had to leave early to ... my cousin at the airport.

A. comings and goings
B. night and day
C. extra-terrestrial beings
D. pick them up
E. such as it was
F. dropped them off
G. meat and drink
H. split my sides laughing
I. unvarnished truth
J. scared out of their wits
K. pick up

The first time

A few years ago, when a couple of old friends invited me to go deer hunting with them in the mountains of New Zealand, I had **mixed feelings**. On the one hand I was excited because hunting was something I had never done before and it seemed like it would be a great adventure. On the other hand, I was very nervous because I had read news reports of how sometimes a **trigger-happy** hunter would fire too soon and accidentally kill another hunter rather than a deer.

It may seem hard to believe, but such things really do happen especially during the time of "the roar". Hunters in New Zealand use that term for the mating season of deer which takes place in April and May, the months of autumn in the Southern Hemisphere. It is called "the roar" because the stags attract hinds, mark out their territory and **warn off** other stags by roaring loudly.

These roars can be heard all over the high country which is **thickly wooded** with forests that the New Zealanders call "the bush". In autumn the weather is usually calm and settled and

The first time

there is a **chill in the air**. It is crisp and cold. Not as cold as it will be in winter but cold enough to remind you that summer is well and truly over. The cold, still air seems to amplify the roaring of the stags and so make it more effective in attracting mates and keeping rivals away.

But it also attracts the hunters because the roar gives them their best opportunity to draw a stag into the open where they can shoot it. They know that if a stag hears the roar of another stag nearby, it will go to investigate and **warn off** the other one or attack it. So, they imitate the roar to entice or lure the stag towards them. Sometimes the hunters' roars are so realistic that other hunters mistake them for deer and, in their excitement, fire without thinking.

Stories like that were **at the back of** my mind as I headed out with my friends Ian and John for a few days hunting. Our destination was one of the huts high in the ranges that are used by trampers in summer and hunters in the autumn. As you would imagine, it was pretty rough. It had two rooms; one was a basic kitchen and the other had bunks for eight people.

We arrived late in the afternoon and settled in. Three of the bunks were already taken but no one was there. They were out hunting, so we made tea and prepared something for our evening meal.

Just before dusk two of the other hunters came in together. One was an old man, I guessed him to be in his late seventies or maybe even 80, and the other was very young. I would guess about 19 or 20 at the most. The old man was very quiet and tired, but the young fellow was **bursting with energy** and excitement. Although they had had a **fruitless day**, he was full of confidence that tomorrow they would get a deer.

He talked fast and he used lots of words that I didn't understand at first although I could pick up the gist of what he was saying. These words were mainly the jargon – the colloquial or technical terms – for things to do with hunting. For instance, he used the word "sign" a lot. "There's lots of sign up there," he said pointing to the high ground behind the hut which was thickly covered in bush. "And there's heaps of sign in the valley beyond, too," he said, waving his arms about.

What did he mean by the word "sign"? Of course, I knew the ordinary or normal meaning of the word, but I had never heard it used in this way before, as an uncountable noun. Usually people refer to "a sign" or "the sign" if they are talking about one or "signs" if they are talking about more than one. But here it was just "sign". Clearly it had some special meaning that all the hunters understood. It was almost as though he was speaking a foreign language.

As the greenhorn in the camp, I didn't want to **show my ignorance** by asking. I was worried that they would think me stupid for not knowing. The only thing I could do was listen carefully and see if I could work out exactly what he meant from the context.

It was pretty obvious that "sign" was something that the deer left behind which would enable the hunters to track them or follow them. But what? My first answer to that question was "droppings" or "dung", the feces or excrement left behind by the deer. One way that hunters stalk their prey is by observing where they have left droppings.

The first time

It seemed like a good answer but the more I listened to the young man, the more I realized there was a lot more to it. "Sign" was a broad term which he used for all sorts of different clues to where the deer had been. It included the droppings but there were other types of sign as well: footprints, tracks, clearings made by the deer and marks on trees where the stags had rubbed their antlers. And then there was the smell. You could smell a stag during the mating season apparently.

There was a whole lot more besides. The young man was a great store of knowledge, a veritable encyclopedia of information about deer hunting. The different types of deer in different parts of the country, the best ways to imitate the roar and a whole host of other things. I was impressed by him and grateful too because John and Ian never said very much. It was as though they assumed that everyone knew everything about hunting just like they did. I could see I wouldn't learn much from them.

The old man didn't say much either, so the young hunter chatted away. He had obviously had an exciting day and had **high hopes** for tomorrow.

"They're roaring all right," he said. "I've never heard such roaring."

It seemed like the young man would never stop talking, he would never run out of new and interesting things to say, observations about deer and the art of hunting them. If I was going to learn anything, it would be from the talkative young man.

But then the last hunter came in from the bush and the young man fell silent. The new man was dressed in camouflage clothing and had his rifle **slung over his shoulder**. The first thing he did when he came into the hut was to unload the rifle, remove all the cartridges to make it safe and then put it away in its case.

Seeing the gun and catching a glimpse of the ammunition, for some reason made me feel nervous again. I had forgotten my worries while listening to the young man talk, he made hunting seem like such a great adventure. But the sight of the gun and the cartridges reminded me of all those stories I had heard about how a day out hunting could sometimes turn into tragedy.

After he had put his rifle away, the new man made something to eat and joined the rest of us, but he didn't say much. In fact, the only thing he offered was that there was a big stag in a valley on the other side of the range and he was going after it tomorrow. He didn't say anything more than that, but his meaning was clear: it was a warning to the rest of us to stay away. That stag was going to be his.

By the time we turned in that night, I had decided that I would not go out with the hunters in the morning. It just seemed too dangerous. The thick bush, the stags roaring and five hunters with high-powered rifles eager to make a kill, to me seemed like an especially perilous mixture.

No, it was **far too risky** for me, so I decided that rather than joining the hunt, I would go tramping, or hiking along the river that ran through the valley below the hut and well away from the danger zone.

In the morning, the hunters set off early up into the hills while I went the other way. I wanted to be as far away from the

The first time

guns as possible and well out in the open so that nobody could possibly mistake me for a deer.

As I walked down the track towards the open ground, I could hear the stags roaring. From a distance they sounded like foghorns: deep and resonant. I **couldn't help but** wonder whether I was hearing the roar of stags or the roar of hunters imitating stags. Certainly, there was no way I could tell the difference.

But by the time I reached the valley floor, the roaring was well **out of earshot**. I couldn't hear it at all. It was quiet and tranquil. The only thing I could hear was the sound of the wind as I walked along the riverbank. At one high point, I looked down and could see a great big trout lazily marking time against the current.

There was no one around so I stripped off and **had a dip** in the freezing cold river. Afterwards, I sat on the bank and had a picnic. I had brought a sandwich and a vacuum flask full of tea.

While I was enjoying the peace and quiet in the early afternoon, I fancied I heard a sharp cracking sound. "Was that a shot?" I wondered. Had one of the hunters got a deer? Or maybe I was just imagining it.

It was time to find my way back and in the late afternoon, as I was heading up the track, I heard another sharp, cracking sound. This time there was no mistaking it. It was a gunshot alright and I **couldn't help but** worry that one of the hunters might have accidentally shot one of the others. But I dismissed the unsettling thought from my mind as soon as it occurred to me. It was better not to think about it.

I was first to arrive at camp, but it was not long before John appeared, carrying the carcass of a hind on his back.

"We'll be having venison for dinner tonight," he declared as he set about skinning it and hanging the meat in a meat safe behind the hut.

After he had put his rifle away and cleaned himself up, we lit the fire and waited for the others.

Ian was next in, but he was empty handed. He had seen a few deer but not in any place that he could get a clear shot.

The old man and the young hunter were next. The old man still silent and looking more tired than ever, his young friend just as excited and as talkative as he had been the night before. He could not stop chattering about all the sign he had seen, all the tracks, droppings, rubbings, scrapings. And the smell! He could smell them everywhere and even hear them although, as yet, had not seen one. Tomorrow would be his day. He was sure of it. He was absolutely confident that one of those stags would be his tomorrow.

Finally, the silent hunter came back carrying the carcass of a magnificent stag on his back.

"What a great set of horns," I said in admiration.

"Antlers," the young man was quick to correct me. "Bulls and cows, goats and sheep have horns," he said, "but deer have antlers." I stood corrected but the young man, as usual, did not pause to let the point sink in. He just kept on talking. He explained that this was a twelve-pointer, meaning that the antlers had twelve sharp points on them. Usually on antlers so large, at least one of the points would be damaged, but this set was perfect. Everything was intact and it would make a fine

The first time

trophy to hang over the mantelpiece or, if the hunter wanted to sell it, he could get good money for it. It would be worth a fortune.

The young man had always seemed a bit shy around the silent hunter. It was as though he was in awe of him. But now, in his excitement, he overcame his shyness and asked where and how the hunter had shot the deer.

The hunter did not say much in reply. He merely told the young man that he had gone over the ridge into a valley where he had killed the stag in the late afternoon. He said nothing more. He gave no details about the hunt, or how he had managed to track the deer or, indeed, the excitement he felt or even whether he had a strong sense of satisfaction from having got such a magnificent trophy.

But the lack of detail from the silent hunter did not bother the garrulous young man who filled the silence with more talking.

"I knew it, I knew it," he said, "I told you the sign was fresh over there. There was sign everywhere."

That night we ate venison cooked on the open fire. In the old days venison was the meat of kings so you could say we ate like kings.

The dinner conversation was once again dominated by the young man chattering away about all things to do with hunting. Now he was comparing the different sounds made by different types of deer during the roar. It was almost as though he was talking to himself, as though he had to express all his inner thoughts out loud.

The others didn't have the same compulsion. On the contrary, they were all quiet, even taciturn. Especially the silent hunter who had shot the stag. But after eating, as we sat in the flickering light of the fire drinking tea out of tin cups, the talk began to flow a little more freely.

During a lull in the conversation, John asked the old man if he remembered when he had shot his first deer. For the first time since we had been there, all the attention was focused on the old man as he reminisced how it was back in the 1930s. He was only a kid, just 14 years old when his father taught him how to hunt. He used his father's old army rifle, a relic of the First World War. But he wasn't hunting for sport or for 12-point trophy heads then. It was the time of the Great Depression, and he did it to put food on the table.

The old man's memories brought a mood of nostalgia into the camp which seemed to loosen the hunters' tongues and one by one they told their stories. Like him, they had all learned the art of hunting from their fathers, and they all did it for food but also the thrill and excitement of the hunt, the skill, being outdoors and in touch with nature and, of course, for the trophy heads as well.

Even the silent hunter told the story of his first deer and for a while they all compared notes about what it had been like and how they had become "hooked" on hunting. But the conversation ran its natural course and began to die down just as the fire was dying down. By the time they all lapsed into silence, the fire was no longer sparking and crackling. And there were no more flames, only glowing embers.

The first time

They were all lost in their own thoughts. But as far as Ian was concerned, it was too soon to turn in for the night, too soon to let the fire go out and too soon to end the conversation. He stood up, got another log and threw it onto the embers which exploded into life with a shower of sparks and crackles and flames.

Then he turned to the one hunter who had not yet told the story of his first deer. The talkative young man who had been dominating so much of the conversation for the past twenty-four hours, had contributed nothing to the reminiscing.

"What about you," said Ian looking at him directly across the flames. "When did you shoot your first deer?"

There was a long pause. The flames danced, the sparks shot up into the night and the faces of the men stood out brightly against the dark sky. All of them turned towards the young man waiting to hear his story.

For what seemed like an eternity he just stared into the fire as though hypnotized. When finally he spoke, he was a complete contrast to the confident, garrulous young man who had greeted us the day before. In a low, soft voice he said, "I haven't shot one yet".

First steps

Fill in the gaps in sentences (1)-(16) with the appropriate idioms from the list below.

(1) For years, the doctors and community leaders have been … drugs but there are always those who pay no attention.

(2) Because of the large number of mass shootings in the United States of America, the country's citizens are getting a global reputation for being ….

(3) There was a ... of reasons why we chose him for the job ahead of all the others. There was his attitude, for a start. He had a very positive outlook and he seemed to be **bursting with energy** to get things done. Then there was his experience. He had lots of experience in this type of role elsewhere and had always achieved great results. And last but not least, he had a solid academic background.

(4) We decided against buying the house even though everything looked good and the builder's report said it was solid. Despite this, ... I had doubts about the structure.

(5) We had ... that the dispute would be settled by the end of the week because most of the points of disagreement had been sorted out.

(6) The politician ... when he mistook the Argentinan President for the Chilean.

(7) You often see images of Santa Claus with a big sack full of presents ....

(8) The company embarked on a risky strategy to try to increase its share of the market. ..., **as it turned out**, because it cost a lot of money but produced very little gain.

(9) A large force of police and emergency service workers spent another ... searching for the boy who had been missing for three days in the **thickly wooded** foothills.

(10) They told us that the land where we went hiking was ..., but we did not realise just how dense the forest was. The trees were so close together that you couldn't see the sky.

(11) There was a ..., so we made sure we were well rugged up with coats and scarves before we went for our evening walk.

The first time

(12) When he was offered the new job, he had …. On the one hand, he would earn much more money which was obviously a good thing. But on the other, he would have to move to a different city away from his family and friends, which was not so good.

(13) After a hard day's physical labour on a hot day, there's nothing better than … in the sea before finishing the day with a splendid dinner.

(14) He was a brilliant footballer but when he injured his knee, the doctors said he would never be able to play again. Sadly, his career was … over.

(15) When they were …, and he knew no one could hear him anymore, he told her what he really thought of his boss.

(16) The children in the playground were …, they were running around, playing games, and making lots of happy noise.

A. mixed feelings
B. trigger happy
C. at the back of my mind
D. fruitless day
E. whole host of
F. high hopes
G. slung over his shoulder
H. Far too risky
I. out of earshot
J. warning people off
K. thickly wooded
L. chill in the air

M. well and truly
N. bursting with energy
O. showed his ignorance
P. having a dip

A bird in the hand

The sign above the shop said, "Al's Antiques" and in a dark room out the back, the owner Al Stokes sat every day waiting for customers and **scrolling through** his social media accounts. Al had opened the shop when he was a young man, but he was **getting on in years** now. He was well into his sixties, and he looked it with his grey beard and long, grey hair tied back in a ponytail.

He dressed in grey too, grey cardigan and old, threadbare, grey slacks. The most colourful thing he wore was a pair of dark red slippers. Everything about Al was untidy, worn out and tired, as if he had **given up on** life. When he had started the shop, he had had dreams of being a prosperous leader of the antiques trade, but he had **fallen well short** of his ambitions and now he faced retirement with nothing to live on except a small government pension.

Although the shop was called "Al's Antiques" it wasn't really an antique shop anymore. It would be better described as a bric-a-brac shop, or a second-hand shop or even just a junk shop. Inside was wall-to-wall clutter, the shop was piled high with bits and pieces of cheap furniture, old cutlery and crockery, tatty books with crinkly pages and torn spines, knick-knacks, costume jewellery and old bottles, walking sticks and hats, mirrors and wardrobes. Where there was space on the walls it was filled with faded old paintings and on the floors, shelves and counters were numerous old clocks that didn't tick anymore as though to remind the customers that, in Al's Antiques, time itself had stopped and the proprietor was going nowhere.

The only thing that really looked like a real antique was an ornate wooden dressing table with a large mirror which sat in a corner. At $3000 it was far and away the most expensive item in the shop and it was also by far the biggest. It had been there for years gathering dust and was obviously much too big and too expensive for Al's customers who were mostly people like him with little or no money.

They came to rummage through the second-hand stuff, the bric-a-brac and the junk hoping to find a bargain. Something cheap and useful or something cheap and attractive, maybe an old piece of jewellery or a nice vase or just a teapot or a knife and fork. They were not the kind of people who would pay $3000 for an old piece of furniture.

But one day a man came into the shop who was unlike Al's usual customers. Whereas they were mostly casually or scruffily dressed, he wore a business suit with a striped tie and polished shoes. As usual, Al put down his mobile phone when he heard the tinkle of the shop's doorbell as the man entered and went to see who had come in. Al observed the man, watching him closely as he rummaged and fossicked and picked his way through the boxes.

"Can I help you?" said Al. "Are you looking for anything in particular?"

"No, I'm fine," replied the man. "Just browsing." And he went on looking at everything in the shop. It wasn't unusual for Al's customers to do this. They often came in and just wandered around for a little while. Sometimes they would buy something if it caught their eye. More often they would leave **empty handed**.

But there was something different about the man in the business suit. For a start, he took more time. He didn't just look at things, he studied them closely. He picked up plates and bowls and vases and looked carefully on their undersides, he held glassware and cutlery up to the light and he examined the dusty paintings both on the front and the back. He didn't seem to be searching for any particular item. He seemed interested in everything.

The last thing he focused on was an old violin which lay among a pile of old musical instruments. He had been in the shop for about half an hour when he picked it up casually. The violin was in very bad condition. It had no strings. The chin rest was cracked. The varnish was chipped and worn and there was a big scratch across the back.

Al couldn't remember when or where had had bought it, but he knew that no one had ever given it so much as a second glance in all the years it had been in the shop gathering dust. So he paid particular attention when the businessman picked it up.

A bird in the hand

At first the man gave it the kind of attention that he had paid to the other pieces. He turned it over in his hands and looked at it closely. It seemed as though he was about to put it back, as he had done with everything else, but then something **caught his eye**. He drew the violin close to his face and peered through the two narrow holes shaped like the letter "f" on either side of the front plate.

He was looking very intently through the holes, carefully studying something. He hesitated for a moment then he switched on the torch of his mobile phone and shone the light inside.

He had obviously found something of great importance because he had been calm before, but now he seemed highly excited. Al was sure that his hands were shaking when he held the violin up with one hand and took photos with his mobile phone in the other. There was something special, something very special about that violin. But what was it?

The man, who hadn't noticed that Al had been watching him, took the violin to the counter and asked about the price.

"How much do you want for this?" he asked.

Although Al was not much of a businessman, he was no fool and had figured out from the man's reaction that the violin must be worth something. So instead of putting a price on it, he **played for time**, he needed to delay the customer so he would have an opportunity to find out why it was so interesting.

"I'm not sure," he said. "I haven't priced it yet."

"Well, I'll give you $5000 for it. Cash," said the man. Al was surprised, in fact he was staggered. He was so shocked that you **could have knocked him down with a feather**. If he sold the violin for that amount of money it would be far and away the biggest sale he had ever made in all his years at Al's Antiques. It was as though he had been told he had won the lottery when he hadn't even bought a ticket. He was so excited he was almost ready to say "yes, you've got a deal".

But then he had **second thoughts**: If the man was prepared to pay so much money for this old piece of junk, then it must be worth far more. The man must have found something that showed the violin was very valuable, but what? He needed more time to find the answer to that question.

"I'll think about it," he said.

"Are you sure?" said the businessman. "I'm offering the money right now, in cash." He was eager, too eager thought Al who stuck to his strategy of **playing for time**.

"No, I'll think about it," he repeated. "Can I have your contact details?"

"How about I give you $7500," said the man. Again, Al was tempted but he **stuck to his guns**.

"No, as I said, I want to think about it. But I promise I'll be in touch."

The businessman handed over his card: "Miles Whitehead, Antiques, Collectables and Fine Art" it said. Mr Whitehead was just the kind of man that Al had always wanted to be, a real antiques dealer.

"I'll be in touch," Al repeated as he **showed Whitehead to the door**.

As soon as Whitehead was gone, Al shut the shop and turned out the lights. Then he took the old violin out to his back room where he shone his mobile phone's light through the f-holes, just as Whitehead had done a few minutes previously.

What he saw made his heart jump. Inside the violin was an old label with the incomplete name Stradivar written on it. Al did not need to be an expert in the history of music to guess what the missing letters were: Stradivarius was the full name. If this was, indeed, a Stradivarius violin, then it would be worth far more than the few thousand dollars Whitehead had offered for it.

Al immediately began researching Stradivarius violins on the internet. **In a nutshell**, what he learned was that Antonio Stradivari was a luthier – or maker of stringed instruments such as violins – from Cremona in Italy who, in the late seventeenth and early eighteenth centuries, became the greatest violin maker in all history. People spoke about their passion for his violins, the richness of the sound they produced, the silvery sweetness of the bright and brilliant tone. For this reason alone, all violinists with ambitions of greatness yearned to possess one, to own one would be like a dream come true.

But Al was not so much interested in the musical qualities of the violin as the numbers. How much might it be worth? The answer was it might be worth millions of dollars. He read that Stradivari had made only 500 violins and about 60 were unaccounted for. It seemed to Al that his dusty old specimen was a missing masterpiece created by the greatest violin maker in history.

The burning question for Al, though, was how much his violin would be worth given that it was in such terrible condition. To find out he took it to the local museum where a young curator examined it.

The museum man was certainly interested although not as excited about the find as Al had expected. He turned it over, ran his eyes over the body of the violin, caressing the wood as though he would be able to divine the truth of its origins through his fingertips and wrinkled his nose when he touched the place where the finish was rough. He held it up to the light and seemed to weigh it in his hands.

Al watched him closely and was practically **bursting with excitement** as the young man finally turned his attention to the f-holes and what lay behind them. Like both Whitehead and Al before him, the young man shone a light into the instrument's dark interior.

After a few moments he carefully put the violin down, but perhaps not as carefully as you would expect of someone handling a million-dollar Stradivarius. He did not give his verdict directly but invited Al to look again at the label. At the bottom, and barely legible, was the word "Germany". Al was puzzled.

"So what?" he said. "The violin was made in Germany. Weren't some of them made in Germany?"

"No, certainly not," said the young man. "Antonio Stradivari made his violins in Cremona," he said, adding "that's in Italy" to emphasise the point.

"So why does the label say it's a Stradivarius," asked Al who was not yet ready to accept what the expert said.

The museum man sighed. He was used to dealing with people who had old pieces of junk which they imagined to be valuable antiques but were really worthless. Just to make sure that Al was **under no illusions** or false hopes about the value of his instrument, he gave him a brief lecture on the history behind Stradivarius violins. Antonio Stradivari, he said, was not only a great violin maker but he also set the shape and dimensions of modern violins. In the nineteenth century violins made in the style of Stradivari were mass produced and these, like the originals, carried the Latin version of his name on their labels: Stradivarius.

"So, they were forgeries … it's a fake, it's counterfeit," said Al who had suddenly **thrown in the towel**. It was not like him to surrender, but he felt he had no choice but to give up in the face of the young expert's confident command of the facts.

"No, not exactly," said the young man. "It was all perfectly **above board**. Everyone at the time knew what was happening. It was part homage to the great man and part marketing tool. The trouble with the violins is that everyone has forgotten about this and so it's **not uncommon** for people to get the wrong idea. Sometimes people coming in who have **jumped to the conclusion** that they've found a million-dollar Stradivarius in the attic or in a junk shop when it's really just a **cheap knock-off** or copy."

So that was it. Far from being worth a million dollars, the dusty old violin was just a cheap imitation worth only a few dollars, if anything at all.

Al wasn't quite beaten yet, though. He still had Whitehead's card and there was the offer of $7500 on the table. So the first thing he did when he returned to the shop was to call

Whitehead. But unfortunately for Al, Whitehead had done his homework too and now he had **changed his tune**.

"A couple of days ago I would have given you $7500 but now I wouldn't give you five cents for that piece of junk," he said. "You should have taken the money when it was offered. Remember the old saying that **a bird in the hand is worth two in the bush**."

First steps

Fill in the gaps in sentences (1)-(19) with the appropriate idioms from the list below.

(1) The government has ... its plan to build another commercial airport. It said project would have cost too much money and it just wasn't worth it.

(2) The shiny object on the beach ... and when he went to investigate, he found that it was a pair of glasses reflecting the sunlight.

(3) He wanted a five per cent pay rise and when they offered him three per cent, he .... Five per cent, he said, or he would find himself another job.

(4) He went fishing for the day, hoping to bring something home for dinner. Unfortunately, the fish weren't biting and he came home ... so we had takeaways that night.

(5) The team on the quiz show had already won $10,000 when they had to make a hard decision. They could take the money or they could risk it all on a final question. If they got the last question right, they would win $100,000 but if they got it wrong, they would lose everything and come away with nothing. In the end, they decided to take the $10,000. When asked why they said, ...

A bird in the hand

(6) Instead of responding immediately to the demand for compensation, the company did nothing. They were … in the hope that the complainant would lose interest.

(7) They moved their son to a new school in the hope that he would do better, but he is not very happy and his academic performance is worse than ever. So, they are having … and might return him to his old school.

(8) When he realised that he had just won the lottery, he was so surprised you ….

(9) You can buy … versions of famous designer brands and electronic equipment. But, of course, it is a false economy. For instance, some say that a knock-off charger can damage your phone.

(10) It was a productive meeting and, when it was over, I …. We shook hands and she set off down the street, disappearing into the crowds of people who thronged the pavement.

(11) The musicians were … that they would get rich playing in pubs and bars. And that's how it was. They got very little money but they really enjoyed themselves.

(12) He wanted to do everything on the cheap, without getting the proper building permits for the job. But we wanted it done …, with everything legal and signed off.

(13) They all sat down at the table for lunch and, after exchanging a few pleasantries, whipped out their mobiles and began … their social media accounts as though the virtual world were more important to them than their companions.

(14) The accused man … overnight, said the detective. "Yesterday, he said he was with friends on Friday when the

murder took place. But now he says he was home alone at the time."

(15) It had been a long running dispute and when we threatened to take the other company to court, they ... and agreed to pay our costs. It was complete surrender.

(16) I don't know why everyone ... that I was guilty. No one ever had any evidence against me. Yet, they still said I was the one to blame.

(17) The woman was ... and wondering whether the time had come to sell her beloved house and move into a retirement village with others of about the same age, in their seventies and eighties.

(18) In the famous novel, *Moby Dick*, Hermann Melville says that it was ... for sharks to follow the whale boats and snap at their oars.

(19) His sales target was 100 units for the month but unfortunately, he ...; he managed to sell only 75.

A. scrolling through
B. getting on in years
C. given up on
D. empty handed
E. playing for time
F. could have knocked him down with a feather
G. second thoughts
H. showed her to the door
I. under no illusions
J. threw in the towel
K. above board

A bird in the hand

L. not uncommon
M. jumped to the conclusion
N. cheap knock-off
O. changed his tune
P. A bird in the hand is worth two in the bush
Q. caught his eye
R. stuck to his guns
S. fell well short

Life's lessons

There comes a time in many people's lives, usually as they are **approaching middle age**, when it feels like there is nothing new and nothing ever changes. "**Been there, done that**" is a common refrain among such people. Every story they hear they have heard before in some form or another and every experience is just a variation of something else that has happened at some other point in their lives. To such people, life can seem like one long cliché. Often, they appear to be tired, bored, cynical or just complacent for want of some novelty in their daily routines.

And yet life still retains a knack of throwing up surprises or shocks that change the game and from which you can learn new and important lessons. I know this because I was one of those been-there-done-that types until the casino came to town.

Everyone was very excited. People were saying that it would **put our town on the map**. We would become a sophisticated tourist destination like Las Vegas or Monte Carlo. Most of us, me included, had never been to a casino and we imagined it

Life's lessons

would be like stepping onto the set of a James Bond movie: men in tuxedos, women in low-cut dresses and bedecked with jewellery and big dollars riding on every spin of the roulette wheel or flip of a card.

For all the excitement, I was not in any great hurry to pay the casino a visit. By this stage, I was happily married and with a family to support. Even though I was in a been-there-done-that frame of mind, there was no way I could afford a **night out** risking the housekeeping money on **games of chance** just for the sake of a little novelty in my life.

But one night I had been on the late shift and missed my usual bus home. I rang my wife to explain and, as I had to wait an hour before the last bus at midnight, to **kill time** I decided to **check out** the casino which was just across the road from the bus stop.

Inside it was not at all as I had expected. No men in tuxedos or glamorous women in expensive frocks. Everyone was dressed casually at best and scruffily at worst.

While there were certainly many people playing roulette and blackjack, by far the most popular method of losing your money in this particular casino was on the poker machines or "the pokies" as they were known. There were rows and rows of them, and all were occupied.

It was more a like a funfair than Monte Carlo, only the lights were much brighter and the prizes were in **cold, hard cash** instead of cuddly toys and candy. And there didn't seem to be much fun in it either.

There was none of the laughter or squeals of delight that you get at a funfair. The dominant sounds were the whirling, whistling and ringing bells of the pokies as they went through their routines.

All the punters seemed hypnotised and gambled in silence with a joyless, mechanical regularity that matched the rhythm of the machines. As soon as one cycle finished, they re-started it. They nearly always came up empty handed but **every now and then** there would be a great clattering noise and the machine would spew out handfuls of chips.

Yet I did not see anyone scoop up their winnings and **quit while they were ahead**. They always fed the chips right back into the machines, mechanically, hypnotically.

While the punters were losing their money, I wandered around the enormous gaming floor – it was as big as a football field – accompanied by the sound effects, the bells and whistles coming from the poker-machine jungle.

At one point, the cacophony was pierced by the sharp wailing of a siren. For a moment I thought that it was a fire alarm. But when I looked around, I saw that it was coming from something that looked like an ice-cream cart with bright, multi-coloured flashing lights. A couple of men dressed up as clowns were hauling it across the vast expanse of the gaming floor. I watched them until they disappeared into the forest of poker machines at the other end leaving me **none the wiser** about their purpose.

By this time, I had seen enough, it was almost a case of sensory overload with all the bright lights and the incessant noise. Just as I was about to leave, I bumped into George McKenzie, an old mate who I hadn't seen for years.

Life's lessons

"**Long time, no see**," we said to each other almost simultaneously and then followed up in unison with a laugh and "**great minds think alike**!"

George was an affable, **hail-fellow-well-met** type of guy who was, typically, on his way to the bar to get himself a beer.

"Join me for a quick one?" he asked.

"Sure, why not." I still had three quarters of an hour before the last bus.

We sat on a couple of stools overlooking the gaming floor, sipping our beer and chatting. George assured me that he didn't come here for the gambling, but it was a great place to get a drink late at night and the beer was cheap.

"It's cut-price beer to tempt the **mug punters** through the door," he said with his trademark cheerful cynicism. That was the thing I liked about George. Although he was a hard-nosed pessimist, he was not at all gloomy.

I remarked to him that the **mug punters**, as he called them, did not look too happy. This was understandable enough when they were losing but, as far as I could see, they didn't look happy when they were winning either.

"That's because they're basically masochists," said George. "There's no pleasing them. They like to feel the pain of losing because it makes them unhappy. But when they win, they still feel unhappy because they miss the pain of losing."

"That's quite a paradox," I said.

"Yep, they're a contradictory lot, these gamblers," said George.

"In other words," I said, "they can't lose because they can't win."

"Precisely," said George.

While we were nutting out the paradoxical state of mind of the average gambler, a young man emerged from the crowd and sidled up to George.

"Hey, George," he said. "You couldn't spare a fag for an old mate, could you?"

"Sure," said George, reaching into his pocket and offering the young man a cigarette and a light.

Jimmy Burrows was the young man's name and he seemed to personify everything we had been talking about. He did not look happy, which is hardly surprising given that he had lost just about all his money. He had enough left for his bus fare home but no more. And yet, he was debating whether to risk it all on one last whirl of the machine. It would be a **last throw of the dice**, as the expression goes, and if it failed, he would have to walk all the way home, a distance of about thirty kilometres.

Despite George's cynicism, he had a kindly heart and tried to persuade his young friend that the bus was by far the best option. But Jimmy had other ideas.

"Nah," he said. "I think I'll give it another go," and he drifted off back towards the poker machines.

"Some people just never learn," said George who gave a **shrug of his shoulders**. He explained that Jimmy had been a barman at the Cherry Tree Hotel, a pub where he used to drink. That was typical George, he knew just about every barman in town.

We picked up the threads of the conversation that Jimmy had interrupted. We had not gone far when we were interrupted again by the wailing siren of one of those brightly lit ice cream carts.

"What's that?" I asked George.

"That's when someone wins big time on the pokies," he said. "Someone over there will have won thousands of dollars and the casino **makes a big fuss of them**."

We raised our glasses to the lucky punter and wondered how much they had won and if it would make them happy. We did not have to wait too long for the answers because moments later, Jimmy rejoined us, grinning from ear to ear.

"Gentlemen," he said, "let me buy you a drink." He was brimming with confidence and a complete contrast to the downcast young man who had been begging for a cigarette only moments before. It was Jimmy who had won big time on the pokies, $20,000 was the prize and he wanted us to help him celebrate.

He embraced us as though we were his oldest and best friends even though I had only just met him, and George was at best merely an acquaintance. We could hardly refuse when he insisted on **shouting us a round of drinks** to help him celebrate.

He bought one round and then another, talking volubly all the time about what he was going to do with the money. He flitted from one idea to another. One moment he was going to buy a car. Another, he was going to put a deposit on a house. He also dreamed of going on a luxury world tour. And he wanted to help his mother out as well, show her a little bit of kindness.

We laughed and teased him, pointing out that, to fulfill all his dreams and plans, would take a lot more than the $20,000 he had just won. Perhaps this was what made him change tack because he stopped talking about how he would spend the money and instead started dreaming about how he could win even more money.

"This is enough dosh to get me into the high rollers room," he said. "It's upstairs and it's where you can win really, really big."

"Yeah," said George. "You might win big, but you are much more likely to do your dough up there."

"Nah," said Jimmy, "I reckon I'm on a streak tonight. I can't lose. I'm going to make a fortune!"

"Don't do it, Jimmy," said George. His tone was a little sharper now. He wasn't joking. "Don't do it, **quit while you're ahead**. The only winner up there is the casino."

But Jimmy wasn't listening. He drained his beer and said, "are you lot coming?" We both shook our heads and Jimmy didn't seem to mind at all. With a cheerful wave he said, "I'm off" and headed over to the lift that would carry him up to the high-roller paradise that he imagined was waiting for him.

"He's a nice guy but a bloody fool too," said George. "Another?"

Before I could say "yes, please" or "no thanks", he took my glass and headed back to the bar for another drink.

About this time, I realised that Jimmy's cameo appearance with his winnings had made me miss the last bus home.

"Oh well," I thought, "I'll get a cab after this."

Life's lessons

But, having allowed George to **shout** me a beer, I was now obliged to **shout** him one back and then he **shouted** me and so on it went into the night. **Shout** for **shout**, drink for drink. The conversation, no doubt, became more and more absurd and we lost all track of time.

Suddenly, I noticed it was six in the morning. Oh my god! I had told my wife I would be on the midnight bus and now it was dawn!

"Gotta go," I said to George and, for once, he did not insist on **one more for the road**. He was ready to **call it a night** as well.

As we were leaving, we bumped into Jimmy at the front door. He had reverted to the downcast young man we had first encountered during the night. The jaunty self-confidence of the big winner was gone. He didn't need to tell us that he had **come a cropper** in the high rollers room and had lost his winnings of the night before, just as George had predicted.

Things were so bad that Jimmy didn't even have his bus fare home. He was preparing for the 30-kilometre trek on foot.

"Go home, Jimmy," said George and gave him five dollars for the fare. Jimmy wandered off into the grey dawn. George and I said our farewells and I crossed the road to the bus stop.

On the bus ride home, I had plenty of time to reflect on the events of the night. My adventure began when I had missed the second to last bus. I had missed the next one as well, thanks to the distractions in the casino. But I had succeeded in catching the one after that, albeit after dawn.

I thought about Jimmy and how sad it was that he had won and lost so much in such a short time. **Easy come, easy go** as they say. And then there was old George. Great company and a great raconteur, he had an amusing story for every occasion. And he was a decent man. He tried to save Jimmy from himself. It wasn't his fault that the lure of easy money had a more powerful influence on Jimmy that George's wise words.

And George could have said "**I told you so**" as we were leaving the casino. But he wasn't that kind of guy. I don't think it would even have crossed his mind.

Maybe there was something about George that gave him some insight and sympathy for the gambler's plight. For it was obvious that George was in trouble himself. What was a middle-aged man doing drinking alone late at night in a casino? He was an alcoholic and perhaps the sufferer of one addiction has a greater understanding of those who suffer from another.

There were definitely some life lessons to be learned from this night at the casino. For Jimmy the obvious one was to **quit while you're ahead**.

As I mused on thoughts like these, I was blithely unaware that the evening held an important lesson for me as well. However, I did not get it until I arrived home to find all my things stuffed into a couple of bags and left on the porch with the front door securely locked.

First steps

Fill in the gaps in sentences (1)-(23) with the appropriate idioms from the list below.

(1) People who win at …, whether cards, dice, roulette or something else, often get **caught up** in the emotion of the moment and imagine that it's all down to their superior skill

Life's lessons

and intelligence. But they are wrong, their success has more to do with luck than anything else.

(2) We had a great … together. First, we went to a show and then we kicked on to a cosy bar for a few drinks and supper before going home.

(3) Once a year they have a gumboot throwing competition in Taihape, a small town in New Zealand. It … for a few days as people come from all round the area take part and join the fun.

(4) The local fish and chip shop told him it would be half an hour before his order was ready. So, to …, he went for a walk.

(5) The new health minister visited the major hospital to … the conditions in the emergency department and to get an understanding of the problems he had to solve.

(6) I did not trust them, so I would not accept payment by credit or debit card. Nothing less than … would do for me.

(7) It doesn't happen very often, but … I get a craving for chocolate.

(8) The politician talked a lot during the interview, but he left us … about whether he was going to resign.

(9) George was an old cynic. When we suggested going on an adventure holiday in the Caribbean, he wasn't at all interested. "…," he said. "I had a great time but wouldn't want to do it again."

(10) It had been a terrific party. Everyone was happy and there was plenty of music and dancing, but Joe had to go to work in the morning, so he decided to … and go home.

(11) Freddy was a real … type. He always seemed pleased to see you and was eager to chat and have a drink.

(12) I warned him not to buy the car but he wouldn't listen. So, when it broke down a few weeks later, I said, "…". As you would understand, he wasn't very happy to be spoken to like this.

(13) They … of her on her seventh birthday. There was a big cake and plenty of balloons and all her friends came round for a big party where they sang Happy Birthday.

(14) "…," said James when he realised that Samantha had made a proposal that was almost identical to his.

(15) It was just before the election and the government was so far behind in the polls that they knew they had to produce something special to have any chance of winning. So, they decided to offer everyone free dental care. It was a bold policy costing billions of dollars and most people saw it for what it was, a ….

(16) A **mug punter** was so excited when he won $500 at the races, that he went out to celebrate. Unfortunately for him, he was picked up for drink driving on the way home and the magistrate fined him exactly $500. As the old saying goes, ….

(17) He took the defeat well. Instead of throwing a tantrum like so many sore losers do, he just …. "You win some, you lose some," he said.

(18) She was … and thought she would never get a starring role again when the film director contacted her and said she would be ideal for his new movie which was about a successful woman in her early forties.

(19) Only once in her life did my mother go to the races and she proved very lucky. She picked every winner for the first few races and had quite a lot of money to bet on the last race.

Life's lessons

Everybody urged her to ..., but she wouldn't listen and put all her money on one last horse. Unfortunately, it didn't win, and she left the track empty handed.

(20) We went to the pub for a quick one. "It's ...," I said, and Andy **shouted** the next one.

(21) "It's getting late," I said. "I really must be going."

"Let's have ...," he said.

"Okay, but just one. I really need to get home."

(22) We warned him not to ride his skateboard down the steep hill but he wouldn't listen. Sure enough, he ... at the bottom and broke his nose.

(23) Thousand of ... lost their money in the online phishing scam.

A. approaching middle age
B. been there, done that
C. puts the town on the map
D. night out
E. games of chance
F. check out
G. cold, hard cash
H. every now and then
I quit while she was ahead
J. none the wiser
K. Great minds think alike
L. hail-fellow-well-met
M. last throw of the dice
N. shrugged his shoulders
O. made a big fuss

P. my shout
Q. one for the road
R. call it a night
S. easy come, easy go
T. I told you so
U. came a cropper
V. kill time
W. mug punters

A piece of advice

When I turned eighteen, I was working as a cadet reporter for a big newspaper. A cadet was like an apprentice, you learned about the craft of journalism on the job in the same way that apprentice plumbers or carpenters learned their trade. Turning eighteen was an important birthday for a trainee journalist, because it meant that you had **come of age**. In other words, you were now an adult and could go to cover stories in places where younger people were not allowed. For instance, seventeen-year-olds were not allowed in pubs or bars and nor were they allowed to go to the racetrack unless accompanied by their parents. The reason for these restrictions was obvious. Alcohol was the big danger in the bars and pubs and gambling at the track.

Of course, the bans only made such places more attractive and exciting to teenagers who couldn't wait to grow up and be treated like adults. I was no exception and so I was very excited when the editor, old Harry Nicholson, called me into his office on the day after my eighteenth birthday to tell me that, now I

A piece of advice

had **come of age**, I was going to help cover the race meetings that were held in our city twice a week on Saturdays and Wednesdays.

Not that I was going to be writing the big, exciting stories with all the important news. On the contrary, I was only going to do the **drudge work**, compiling the detailed results of every single horse race run in our city. Not just which horse came first, second and third but everything from first to twenty-third and including such things as the odds, the names of trainers, jockeys, previous results of the horses, how much weight they carried in handicap races and so on.

After giving me my assignment, old Harry offered me one piece of advice: "**If I were you** I'd remember that there's only one rich racing writer in this town and that's our own Bob Truman," he said and after pausing for emphasis he added: "and he inherited his money from his parents." I wasn't quite sure what he meant at first. Bob Truman was the chief racing reporter at our newspaper, the *Morning Herald*. **When it came to** racing, he was regarded as about the best journalist in the country and yes, I suppose you could call him rich from what I knew of him. Certainly, he drove a nice car and was always smartly dressed in expensive-looking suits.

I asked an older reporter what Harry meant, and he just laughed. "He says that to all the youngsters he sends to the track," he said. "He's warning you not to succumb to temptation and waste your money gambling. And he's right. It's a **fool's game**. You might strike it lucky on one day but, **in the long run**, you always lose if you **give in to** temptation."

"Oh, I get it," I replied although I didn't really **grasp the full extent of** what he meant. That would come later.

In the meantime, I had to **come to grips with** my new job. **Learning the ropes** was really stressful. There was so much excitement and energy at the track. Everyone seemed in a hurry and no one had much time to explain things to the **new kid on the block**.

But basically, it went like this. All the journalists worked together in a big room underneath the grandstand. They all had their own places on a big desk where they would write their reports. At one end of the room was a special café for the press which served afternoon teas and the most fabulous cream-cake selection I had ever seen in my life. But on that first day I didn't have any time to enjoy it, I was so busy **learning the ropes** of my new job.

A race was run about every half an hour, and we all trooped up a steep ladder into the press box in the stand to watch. Afterwards there would be a mad rush as some reporters went off to interview the jockeys and trainers while others started writing their reports and I had to compile what seemed like bewildering sets of facts, figures and names into tables ready for publication in Monday's newspaper.

One of the things I remember most about those days was the noise. From the stand you could hear the sound of the horses' hooves as they thundered past the winning post. The reporters always talked loudly, almost **shouting**, the clatter of typewriters, the ring-ring-ringing of the telephones, the chattering of the teleprinters. And there was a lot of swearing and cursing as well.

A piece of advice

Things seemed to go wrong a lot, mistakes were made and, before too long, I realized that as often as not, money was being lost as well.

One especially noticeable loser was Neville Lovecock, known to everyone as "Nifty" which was a word which used to mean smart, stylish or fine but had been adapted as the standard nickname for anyone called Neville. It must be said, Nifty Lovecock was anything but smart, stylish or fine. On the contrary, he was a large, scruffy **thick-set** man whose style would be best described as **op-shop** or **thrift shop** if you were in the United States. His suit was always crumpled. In fact, he looked as though he slept in it.

He was middle aged and seemed both angry and sad. As a senior journalist who wrote his reports for the *Evening Star*, he ignored me, he had no reason to speak to the most junior person in the place, especially one who worked for a rival paper. But then again, he didn't have to say anything for me to figure out what was going on. He did a lot of swearing and after every race he came into the office and took some betting slips out of his pocket, tore them up and chucked them under his chair.

By the end of every meeting, Nifty was sitting on top of a small mountain of scrap paper, and this was what helped me understand fully the meaning of old Harry's piece of advice.

In the meantime, I settled in and quickly **got the hang of it**. I became so efficient that I usually compiled all the details and statistics within minutes of a race ending and this gave me plenty of time to drift down to the café and sample the afternoon teas. I must say they **lived up to** expectations and, what is more, they were free. You didn't have to pay a cent.

There were three racetracks in the city and each one had its own specialities. At the River track, which was where I first went, there were endless supplies of cream cakes, chocolate eclairs **to die for**, Boston buns and lamingtons. At the new track there was angel food cake, coffee cake and the most divine tiramisu. Then there was the Valley, they had caramel cakes, chocolate cakes, cheesecakes of every imaginable variety, Pavlovas, cupcakes, muffins and, to top it all off, Sacher torte. I could never make up my mind which spread I preferred. They were all great.

What's more, the cakes never **ran out**. It seemed there was an endless supply. No matter how much I ate there was always more; an invisible reservoir of rich cakes hidden somewhere behind the counter.

I **couldn't help but** wonder whether the free cakes, plus generous supplies of beer, whisky and wine, explained why all the senior reporters were so big. To put it politely, they were large men. Some people might say they would be better described as "solid" or "stocky" or, to be really frank, maybe even obese. Some of them were almost as broad as they were tall. They looked square and it was an impression reinforced and emphasized by the fact that nearly all of them wore double-breasted suits.

Suits like that, with their two rows of buttons on the front, wide lapels and broad shoulder pads, were very much the fashion in those days. At the racetrack, they were almost like a uniform among the pressmen who all came to work wearing hats as well, mostly trilbys and fedoras just like in the old

A piece of advice

gangster movies. On one arm they carried their binoculars and in the opposite hand, their guides to the day's racing program.

Every Saturday and every Wednesday for the next year, I joined them at the races. I watched every race and after each one I dashed down to the press room to write up the details. And in between times, I made the most of the racetracks' hospitality and ate as many cream cakes as I could.

There were only two things that broke the routine. The first was on the big Cup Day. The biggest race of the year and many reporters from other cities and even other countries came to cover the big event. Things were noisier than ever before and at times it got quite tense.

It was in this tense atmosphere that Nifty Lovecock spoke to me for the first time. He desperately needed to clarify some facts in a report he was writing about the big race, and I was the only person who had the full details.

"Young fella," he said, "you wouldn't be able to lend me a copy of your details, would you? I really need to check something." He was trying to sound friendly but could not completely hide the fact that he was nervous. This was hardly surprising given that I worked for a rival newspaper and that he had studiously avoided speaking to me for some months as though I was beneath him. Now that he needed something from me, now that he wanted me to do him a favor, he was being **as nice as pie**.

I could have **told him where to go**, but I'm not like that. I'm not a rude, aggressive person and, what's more, I find it very hard to say no. It was **no skin off my nose** to give him the details. I wouldn't lose anything or suffer any disadvantage by helping him. So I gave him a copy and he thanked me very much. From then on Nifty would at least acknowledge me when he saw me although he still didn't say much.

But a few weeks later, he broke the routine for the second time when he came over to me in the press room with some advice of his own.

"I've got a tip for you, young fella," he said. "Out and About in the fourth race today. It's at **long odds**, 100 to one and I'm told it's just about certain to win. I'm **putting a packet on it** and **if I were you**, I'd do the same."

That was it. That was all he said. The odds meant that for every dollar you bet on it you would get a hundred back. He didn't tell me how much money he was betting but it was a lot. He was very excited and very nervous, and it rubbed off on me. I **couldn't help** doing the calculations myself. A hundred dollars back for every one invested! Ten dollars gets you a thousand! Twenty dollars gets you two thousand! A hundred dollars gets you $10,000.

Wow! That was a lot of money. A huge sum. I would have had to work for years to earn that amount. Very briefly I thought about old Harry Nicholson's piece of advice about Bob Truman being the only rich racing writer in town. But the thought of $10,000 outweighed it by far. It would be the easiest money I would ever make. So, I went down to place my bet and my hand trembled as I passed the $100 over, equivalent to about four weeks' pay at the time.

I then took my place in the press box to watch the race. In all the months I had been doing this job I had learned to watch carefully and note where all the horses were placed at different

A piece of advice

stages. But this time I had eyes only for the 100-to-one shot, Out and About whose jockey wore black and yellow.

It was a long race and Out and About started well enough, about the middle of the field. You did not want your horse to lead at the start because it would almost certainly **run out of** breath in the home straight and be passed by other horses.

But there was a risk that a horse **in the middle of the field** would be boxed in and therefore would not get a chance to take the lead. And that's what seemed to be happening to Out and About as I watched him through the binoculars on the far side, galloping along the back straight.

As the horses turned into the home straight, though, he suddenly got his chance. It seemed that some of them ran wide, opening up a big gap in the middle and Out and About with the unmistakable yellow and black colors of his jockey, charged through that gap. You could hear the crowd roar and suddenly we were all on our feet cheering him on, even in the press box. The unthinkable was happening, the long shot was going to win the race.

And so he did. He won it comfortably in the end and I have never been as happy and elated as I was when he thundered across the finish line with all the other horses strung out behind him.

I was $10,000 richer but I still had to finish my days' work and I couldn't stop my hand from shaking. When I got the chance, I went over to old Nifty Lovecock and thanked him for the tip. I **couldn't help but** notice that, for the first time since I had been going to the races, there were no torn-up betting slips under his chair.

And that was the last I ever saw of him. Rumors were swirling around about how much money had been won on Out and About. Some said Nifty had made enough money to recoup all his losses in a lifetime of gambling. Others complained the race had been rigged, or fixed. That is to say, someone had cheated. Maybe they had an agreement to let Out and About through the gap so that he could win. But **nothing ever came of it** as far as I knew, and nobody ever questioned me about where my new-found wealth came from.

The first thing I did with my winnings was to buy a decent suit. The one I had was pretty shabby, so I went along to an expensive men's clothing store. I thought I may as well wear the same uniform as all the other the men of the racetrack, so I tried on a double-breasted suit. It was too small for me. It seemed I had put on quite a bit of weight in the past few months. So, I tried on a suit that was a couple of sizes bigger.

As I looked at myself in the changing room mirror, I **couldn't help but** notice how much I had changed. I had been a skinny kid but now I was solid, even stocky and the double-breasted suit made me look square, just like all the old journalists at the racetrack. In the light of my $10,000 win and the way I had stacked on the weight, I **couldn't help** thinking that Harry had given me the wrong advice. Perhaps it would have been better if he had told me to stay away from the cream cakes.

First steps

Fill in the gaps in sentences (1)-(24) with the appropriate idioms from the list below.

(1) He was a great mathematician but … picking winners at the racetrack, he was hopeless.

A piece of advice

(2) I have finished the painting and it's … whether you like it or not. What's important to me is what the art-loving public thinks.

(3) At some point, all language learners have to … the grammar of their new language if they want to succeed.

(4) Many people often fail to … the health hazards that can arise from smoking and drinking too much alcohol. It's not just that those things make you feel bad in the morning, they do lasting damage to your body and, in the end, they can kill you.

(5) Some people say love is a …, others use the expression to describe any form of gambling.

(6) Too many people insisting on buying new things when, assuming you really want to do your best for the environment, you should go to …, where you find second-hand goods of excellent quality and style, everything from clothing to household furniture. It's the original way of recycling.

(7) The … was pretty smart. It didn't take him long to **learn the ropes** of his new job.

(8) As soon as the school athletics coach saw the … young man he knew that he would be a good weightlifter.

(9) In the old days, your 21st birthday party was special because 21 was when you …. That is, you could vote in elections, drink alcohol, drive cars and get married without your parents' consent. Now, in most countries, you can do all of these things long before you turn 21.

(10) When he first started working with computers, he thought it was all very strange and difficult but after a while, he … and now everything is so easy it's almost like second nature.

(11) We had a fabulous dinner at the Italian restaurant. She had the pasta, and I had the chicken and for dessert we shared a panna cotta which was ….

(12) The car … petrol on the motorway. It was so embarrassing; I had forgotten to fill it up.

(13) …, I'd buy a new computer. This one is on its last legs.

(14) He had cheated on his girlfriend and they broke up. After a while, he realized that she was the one he really wanted and tried to get back together with her. But she was still angry with him and ….

(15) The Government had ambitious plans to build a light rail track all the way from the CBD to the airport, but …. We still make that trip by bus or taxi.

(16) When George started his new job at the hamburger bar, they assigned an experienced worker to help him ….

(17) Some investors say real estate is the most profitable place for their money, for others it is bank deposits, but others say that, …, you get a better return on your money by investing in the stock market.

(18) After a full day of negotiations, the government was still refusing to … the demands of the protesters.

(19) She had hoped for something better when the restaurant hired her, but the job was …, mainly washing dishes and scrubbing floors. It was physically hard and repetitive and so boring it was hard to stay focused even though it required little or no thought or initiative.

(20) I'm so confident that my team is going to win the cup that I'm ….

A piece of advice

(21) After the building collapsed in a big earthquake, the authorities said it was … that they would find anyone alive in the rubble.

(22) Her manager told her she would be fired if she continued being rude to the customers. After that, she was … to everyone; she really needed that job.

(23) I … how pale the man looked. And no wonder, **it turned out** he was having a heart attack.

(24) The boy finished the race …, fifth out of ten.

A. came of age
B. drudge work
C. when it came to
D. fool's game
E. in the long run
F. give in to
G. grasp the full extent of
H. come to grips with
I. learn the ropes
J. new kid on the block
K. thick-set
L. op-shops or thrift shops
M. got the hang of it
N. to die for
O. told him where to go
P. no skin off my nose
Q. long odds
R. putting a packet on it
S. If I were you

T. nothing ever came of it
U. as nice as pie
V. ran out of
W. couldn't help but notice
X. in the middle of the field

Taken for a fool

You should never judge a book by its cover is an old saying that is full of wisdom but, unfortunately, is usually **honoured in the breach**. If anyone ever tells you they never judge people by appearances, then you can be sure that they are not telling the truth.

I know this because, like everyone else, I do it all the time, even though I know I shouldn't. For example, when I first met Frank Brower and Kate Smith, I immediately **jumped to the conclusion** that there was something very odd about them.

Frank was a small man with the typical signs of **approaching middle age**, the **receding hairline**, the thinning grey hair and the **thickening waist**. Kate, on the other hand, was much younger, in her early twenties. She aspired to be a top fashion model and, I must say, she fitted the stereotype being tall, slender and blonde with the most **striking blue eyes** I had ever seen.

Taken for a fool

Her youthful bloom only served to make Frank look older, smaller and less significant. It was a bit like a flamingo dating a sparrow.

The appearances made me think that there must be more to this relationship that just love. The other element, of course, would have to be money. I did not know at the time what Frank did for a living but gathered that he was some sort of senior executive and trouble shooter at one of the top corporations in the country.

You only had to see his shiny sports car to guess there was money behind him. And, although we lived in the same block apartment building, his place was much bigger than mine and lavishly furnished in contrast to my **spartan digs** where a couple of sticks of second-hand furniture were all I could afford.

What's more, he had a liquor cabinet that was always well stocked with the most expensive brands, especially single-malt Scotch whisky. He loved a **wee dram** in the evening, did Frank. And on special occasions he would happily **pop the corks** on bottles of Champagne.

But as I got to know my neighbours better, I began to doubt that money was really the great motivator in their relationship as I had first thought. They seemed perfectly in tune with one another with shared interests.

Style and fashion were important to them both. Not only were they smartly dressed in pricey looking clothes, but the apartment was luxuriously furnished with all the **mod cons**. They never stopped reminding their guests that the television and all their many kitchen appliances and gadgets, as well as their heating and cooling systems, were the best that money could buy.

And the food! They were great cooks, as I found out one Saturday night when they invited me over for dinner to meet some of their friends.

They served a four-course meal that would not have looked out of place in a five-star restaurant. It was so good that it was an obvious conversation piece with the other guests, among whom was a **professional couple** who were dedicated foodies.

They savoured every mouthful and analysed each dish with the attention to detail you would expect from a food critic on The New York Times. And when they were not talking about the food everyone nattered happily about the inconsequential things in life. Fashion, as you would expect, house prices, beach holidays and places they had been to, things they had seen as tourists.

No one talked about books or politics or art except Frank who laughingly said he had been to the Louvre once and as far as he was concerned, it was just one damn painting after another.

The party broke up just before midnight and everyone declared it a great success. We parted with promises that we would all do it again soon. This was the beginning of a pattern in my life. Frank and Kate **took me under their wing**. They were determined to make a thoroughly modern young man out of me. I had always been a shabby dresser, but they took me out shopping for new clothes and insisted on an expensive haircut to update my "look".

Taken for a fool

It was bemusing to me, but I went along with it. I began to imagine that appearances did matter; that how you dressed somehow had everything to do with success in the real world. Maybe Frank and Kate really did know the secret for a happy and contented life. Wouldn't it be nice, I thought, to have everything as well sorted as they did.

Having **smartened me up**, they continued to issue dinner invitations and take me to parties. I **couldn't help but** notice there were always young, single women on every occasion and, naïve though I was, I was not so naïve that I couldn't figure out what was going on.

I didn't mind a bit, though. On the contrary I really liked the idea of finding a girlfriend. But it never seemed to happen. Frank and Katie's friends just didn't gel with me or, perhaps more realistically, I didn't gel with them.

Yes, I think the latter was more likely. I was a rather earnest young man who read weighty books and was struggling to come to terms with the ways of the world and the meaning of life. Frank, Kate and their friends, by contrast, were as light as feathers as they floated over the topics that most interested them, fashion, gossip and the latest TV reality shows.

Not really my cup of tea, although I was happy to go along with it at the time.

Never did I think that the friendship would endure in the long term, but nor did I imagine that it would end as abruptly as it did. The end came at a dinner party given to welcome home a couple who had been living in New York at the time of the 9/11 terror attacks.

For once, the conversation at Frank and Kate's drifted on to more serious subjects as they told us what it was like to be in the Big Apple on that terrible day. I was certainly eager to hear their stories but, before they had gone very far, Kate interrupted and declared loudly and confidently that 9/11 was a **false-flag attack** and that it was all a conspiracy by the CIA.

The other guests were stunned into silence by Kate's sudden and uncharacteristic sortie into international affairs. I was the only one foolish enough to challenge her but whatever I said, she just batted away with the assurance of someone who had no room for doubt in her mind.

As the verbal jousting progressed it became more and more tense and, along the way, Kate revealed herself to be an arch-conspiracy theorist. Not only did she believe that 9/11 was planned and executed by the government, but she also believed in just about every other conspiracy theory circulating on social media from the assassination of John F. Kennedy in 1963 to the belief that the world is run by lizard people from outer space who have disguised themselves in human form.

This was too much for me. I laughed in her face. "Surely, you don't believe that rubbish," I said. "Only a fool could believe that."

There was an uncomfortable silence. Kate was suddenly lost for words but the expression on her face said it all. The edges of her mouth were turned down and she looked as though she might burst into tears, although they were not tears of sorrow that she was holding back, but tears of rage.

"Don't you dare **take me for a fool**," she hissed through **gritted teeth**.

Taken for a fool

From that moment, the friendship was over. The invitations to parties and dinners stopped and, even though we still lived in the same apartment block, somehow our paths never crossed anymore. I did see Frank from time to time, but he always seemed embarrassed. He avoided eye contact and would hurry away after the briefest of greetings.

Eventually I moved to another part of town and found other friends. It was surprising how quickly Frank and Kate faded from memory. But they were not out of my life altogether. In time, each would reappear.

Frank was the first. I was taking a coffee break at work one morning and browsing the paper. On an inside page was the headline, "Clerk gets two years for fraud". Normally, I wouldn't spend too much time on such a trivial story, but the name of the clerk caught my eye: Frank Brower.

Frank, **as it turned** out, was not quite the successful businessman that I had taken him to be. He was a relatively lowly office worker in large retail chain who had been embezzling, that is stealing, money from his employer for years. By the time they caught him, he had fleeced large sums of money from the company.

He was motivated by pure greed, said the judge, and the money went on supporting an extravagant lifestyle that would otherwise have been well beyond his means.

He mentioned the flashy cars, the expensive restaurants and the champagne but spared Kate the embarrassment of mentioning her by name. Nevertheless, there was only one possible conclusion for me to draw. Kate and Frank's relationship had really been about money, after all.

Poor Frank, he had tried to buy love only to find that he couldn't afford it. It seemed from the newspaper report that Frank was all alone when he faced his destiny in court: two years in prison with the possibility of parole in one year for good behaviour.

As it turned out, it was about a year later when it was Kate's turn to resurface in my life. Again, I was sitting at my desk feeling a little drowsy after lunch one day when the phone rang. It was Kate and the contrast with the last time we had met could not have been more **striking**. Gone was the sullen, angry, icy tone and instead she was all warmth and friendship.

"**Long time, no see**," she said. "We really ought to **catch up** soon."

"Sure," I said, "that would be great," but not feeling all that enthusiastic about the idea.

"It's really important," she said, perhaps detecting the lack of enthusiasm in my voice. "You're a **man of the world** and I really need your advice about something super important."

I was not enough of a **man of the world** to resist the flattery and I was hooked.

"My advice? About what?"

"I've been offered the chance to make a lot of money in a fantastic investment and I wanted to discuss it with you. The returns are really, really good but I wanted to talk to someone about it first and I thought you would be the best person to give advice, you being a **man of the world** and all that."

"When you say the returns are fantastic, what do you mean exactly?" I asked.

"Well, twenty to twenty-five per cent per month, guaranteed," she said.

"Per month!"

"Yes, per month."

"That's impossible," I told her clearly and firmly trying as hard as I could to sound like a real **man of the world**. "It sounds too good to be true and you know the old saying …"

"What old saying?" she asked.

"If it sounds too good to be true, it probably is."

It took a while for the meaning of this to register with Kate but when she realised what it meant, she protested.

"No, no, no, this opportunity is different, it's legit."

"So why do you need my advice?"

"I just want to be certain," she said. "Look, there's a meeting for potential investors tonight. Please come and listen to what they have to say. I'd be really, really grateful."

The combination of Kate's flattery and my own curiosity persuaded me to go even though there was obviously something dodgy going on.

It was well after nightfall when I arrived at the suburban community hall where the meeting was to be held. As I walked down the street, I could see the lights of the hall glowing in the distance and I was conscious that many other people, shadowy figures in the dark, were heading in the same direction. We were like the faithful flocking to hear the wise words of some religious guru or prophet, only our purpose had much more to do with earthly wealth than the world of the spirit.

There were sixty or seventy people **milling around** outside the hall and in the foyer. Most of them had grey hair and looked as though they might have plenty in their retirement funds.

Inside the auditorium, workers were still setting up the rows of portable chairs in front of a low stage which had a lectern and a large screen for projecting facts, figures and important information aimed at persuading the audience to part with their money.

Among the workers was a small, grey-haired man. Was it Frank? It certainly looked like him and he would have been out of jail by now. But as I only caught a glimpse of him, I couldn't sure. In any case, before I had the chance to approach him, Kate appeared.

She thanked me warmly for coming and then, looking around her suspiciously and, speaking in a low, nervous voice, she asked me if I had a cigarette.

"Why sure," I said, reaching into my pocket,

"No, no, not here," she whispered. "He doesn't like me smoking."

"Frank? He never minded before," I said.

"No, not Frank, Robert."

"Who's Robert?" I asked.

"The owner of the company," she said.

We moved outside and around the corner and out of sight of the hall where she eagerly accepted my offer of a cigarette. She dragged on it greedily and the glow bathed her face in an eerie red light. She looked drawn and anxious.

She explained to me that she was no longer with Frank but was going to marry Robert.

Taken for a fool

I told her I thought I had seen Frank in the hall, and she confirmed that it was him. He was there doing what he could to help out. Everything was cool between them, and Robert was a really great guy.

"Only he doesn't like you smoking," I said. "What will he say if he finds out?"

"He'll be really angry," she said. "It really **pisses him off**. It's the one thing he really, really hates."

"Aren't you worried that he'll smell it on your breath?"

She just **shrugged**. She finished her smoke and dropped the butt on the pavement and extinguished it with a twisting motion of her foot. It was time to go inside.

All the old people were shuffling along and taking their seats. The hall was filled with the murmur of whispered conversations. When the lights went down the murmur was hushed. All was quiet except the occasional cough and rustle of paper as the audience waited for the show to begin.

Robert kept them waiting for two or three minutes before stepping out onto the stage and into the spotlight. He introduced himself and then begin his spiel with a series of questions.

"Have you ever wondered why some people are so rich? How do they do it? What is their secret?"

And, of course, he had all the answers. He promised to share the secret which he had discovered years before and was now eager to reveal.

By way of reinforcing his point, he used the big screen to illustrate a series of personal stories of ordinary people – people just like those in the audience – who had joined his scheme and made their fortunes. The battlers had become **comfortably off** and the **comfortably off** had become wealthy thanks to him.

Then he explained how it was done, through a deep understanding of the markets and how they fluctuated he was able to show that his scheme consistently produced returns of between twenty and twenty-five per cent per month.

Lots of facts and figures flashed up on the big screen and almost everyone in the audience was leaning forward trying to absorb as much of the information as they possibly could, some were even scribbling notes.

Robert urged them to put as much cash as they could spare into the scheme. You will not find a better opportunity anywhere, he assured them. What's more, he was guaranteeing the returns so there was no need to heed warnings about **putting all your eggs into one basket**.

"With this investment you cannot fail. If ever there was a **pot of gold at the end of the rainbow**, this is it."

The great thing about Robert was that he came across as a good, generous man. He had found the secret to making a fortune and, instead of keeping it all to himself, he wanted everyone to spread the word.

"Tell as many people as you can," he urged the audience. "Get all your friends to join in. The more investors we have, the greater the profits."

At the end of his presentation, Robert directed anyone who was interested in taking advantage of his fantastic offer to sign up at the long row of tables running down the side of the hall. Among the clerks taking down the details was the small, grey-haired man. It was, indeed, Frank!

Taken for a fool

I didn't get the chance to talk to him, however, because he was **far too busy**. The people in the audience had been spellbound by the force of Robert's presentation and the promise of the fortunes that awaited them. They besieged the tables and Frank and his co-workers were so busy there was simply no chance of chatting to him.

But Kate sought me out in the happy crowd. She was **hanging out for** a cigarette again and asked if she could have another one.

"Of course," I said, and we retreated outside once more. I lit her cigarette and simultaneously gave her the benefit of my advice.

"It's a scam, a Ponzi scam to be exact," I said, "and I wouldn't have anything to do with it **if I were you**."

"A what?"

"A Ponzi scam. It's one of the oldest scams in the book. You are sucked in by the offer of impossibly high returns from someone who says they have unlocked the great secret of untold riches."

"What's wrong with that," Kate protested. "Robert has worked out the secret and he does pay twenty to twenty-five per cent a month. I know because I invested all my savings and I'm making lots and lots of money. You don't know what you're talking about."

"Exactly," I told her. "And I bet he's told you that you have to recruit as many new investors – or should I say mugs – as you possibly can."

"Yes, of course. You heard Robert, the more people who invest, the more we can grow the pie. It's a win-win situation."

"No, it's not," I was trying to bring her back down to earth. "You have to recruit new people because the new investments are what is paying the interest on the old investments. That's all there is to it. Despite what Robert says, there is no secret investment strategy beyond this. It's a scam and the danger for you and the others is that, as soon as the new investments dry up, the whole thing will collapse. It's fraud, it's criminal."

Kate was unmoved. She laughed in my face.

"What nonsense," she said. "I'm getting rich from this, and you could too if you weren't such a fool."

I recognised the same hard expression on her face that I had seen all those years before when we fell out over her conspiracy theories.

"Well, if you've already put your money in and you're so convinced, what did you want my advice for?" was my response.

It was extremely naïve of me under the circumstances. Of course, she didn't want my advice, she wanted my money. To her, I was not a **man of the world** at all, I was just another mug. Her aim all along had been to get me to the meeting so I could be sucked in to the scam like everyone else.

Thankfully, it was dark, so I don't think she noticed how I blushed when I realised that, this time, I was the one being **taken for a fool**.

First steps

Fill in the gaps in sentences (1)-(26) with the appropriate idioms from the list below.

(1) Ol' Blue Eyes was the nickname of the famous singer, Frank Sinatra on account of his ....

Taken for a fool

(2) On the day of the big airline strike, we arrived at the airport to find thousands of people … in the terminal looking lost.

(3) When he was young, the rock star had long wavy hair that often covered his eyes, especially when he was performing. But now he has grown old, his … and you can see his forehead.

(4) The Smiths were not rich nor were they poor, they were …. They had enough money to cover all their expenses and could afford to travel overseas for their holidays every year.

(5) When we first saw the house, we fell in love with it. From the outside it looked perfect but when we went inside, we saw that it was in very poor condition. The walls were damp and dirty, the fittings were broken and there was rubbish all over the place. It just goes to show that ….

(6) When I first came to London, I lived in … with just one room, a bed, a kettle for making tea or coffee and there was a shared bathroom down the hallway.

(7) The company had a policy of putting its customers first, but this was usually … as it always gave priority to its own interests.

(8) In his younger days, my father was a doctor in the Highlands of Scotland. He used to make house calls and he remembers one patient who, after the consultation, would always bring out a bottle of the finest Scotch whisky from under his bed and invite Dad to linger for a ….

(9) He was a real …: he was sophisticated, had experience in highly demanding executive roles, was well educated and well-travelled. He could converse authoritatively on a wide range of

topics, as well as business and the economy, he knew a lot about the arts and sciences. To top it all off, he spoke three languages.

(10) He was really ... because the goods he had ordered did not arrive on time.

(11) It was a fabulous New Year's Eve party. They ... just before midnight and everyone welcomed the new year in the best possible style.

(12) My neighbours were always dreaming of striking it rich. They thought that one day, they would find the ..., maybe by winning the lottery or maybe some rich relative would leave them lots of money in his will.

(13) Their new kitchen had all the ...: an air fryer, a microwave, an espresso machine, an ice cream maker and many more interesting gadgets.

(14) The real estate advertisement said the townhouse for sale near the city centre would suit a .... Bob, who was a surveyor, and Mary, who was a lawyer, thought it would be ideal for them.

(15) The captain of the football team ... to help him settle in a get to know his new teammates.

(16) I've known Fred for many years. When I first met him, he was slim, but now, as he has grown older, his .... As well as old age, the cause of this change was, no doubt, too many pies and too much beer.

(17) Mary prefers bland food. She once tried eating a very hot curry, but it was .... She didn't like the spicy flavour and, no matter how much water she drank, she could not stop the burning sensation in her mouth.

Taken for a fool

(18) I bumped into an old workmate in the street the other day. He looked very well but we did not have much time to chat, so we agreed that we should ... for a coffee next week.

(19) The old man was having trouble looking after himself. His clothes were in very bad condition, his trousers had holes in them, and his shirts were frayed at the edges. He had not shaved in weeks and his thinning grey hair was long and straggly. His family decided they had to do something to help him, so they set about ...: they bought him new shirts and trousers and took him to the barber for a haircut and a shave.

(20) The politician told too many lies and made too many promises that he could not fulfil but the voters saw through him. They did not like being ... and he lost the election by a wide margin.

(21) The destruction of the space station was a .... Everyone assumed at first that it was done by the Galaxy Alliance. But later investigations showed the real perpetrators were their enemies, the Solar System rebels, who made it appear as though the Alliance was responsible.

(22) It had been such a busy morning that she had not had time to eat or drink so by 11am she was ... a cup of coffee. As soon as she satisfied her craving for caffeine, she knew everything would be better.

(23) Any financial adviser worth their salt will tell you that you shouldn't .... If you do, and the basket is dropped, you will lose everything.

(24) The children were fighting all day, there was lots of screaming and **shouting** and each one blamed the other for starting it. Eventually, their mother lost patience and, through

..., told them to stop it and to go to their rooms until they decided to improve their behaviour.

(25) Everyone thought the team was weak but, ..., they had hidden strengths and won the championship.

(26) They had been best friends at school, but they went their separate ways afterwards. Years later, they bumped into each other at the airport. "...," they said.

A. you can't judge a book by its cover
B. honoured in the breach
C. hairline is receding
D. waist has thickened
E. striking blue eyes
F. spartan digs
G. wee dram
H. popped the corks
I. mod cons
J. professional couple
K. took the new player under his wing
L. smartening him up
M. not her cup of tea
N. false-flag attack
O. taken for fools
P. gritted teeth
Q. catch up
R. man of the world
S. pissed off
T. comfortably off
U. put all your eggs in one basket
V. pot of gold at the end of the rainbow

Taken for a fool

W. hanging out for
X. long time, no see
Y. milling around
Z as it turned out

A date to remember

I met Eva in Buenos Aires, but I didn't know her very well, so I was surprised one day when she suggested we **go out on a date**. Now, before you **jump to conclusions**, I would not want you to **get the impression** that this was a romantic date. On the contrary, it was **nothing of the kind**.

You see, Eva, who was from Denmark, had been backpacking around North and South America for a year and now it was time for her to return home. It was her last night in Buenos Aires, and she thought it would be nice to go out for dinner but she had no one to go with.

We were both staying at a backpackers' hostel in a street called Alsina, not far from the Plaza de Mayo and, as it happened, I was the only person in the hostel who was free for a date that night. All the others either had something to do or already had partners. So naturally I was **only too happy to oblige**.

What better place to farewell a continent than the famous Buenos Aires suburb of San Telmo, which was only a few blocks

A date to remember

from where we were staying? It is the oldest neighborhood in the city and is renowned for its grand colonial architecture, its fabulous antiques markets and its bars and cafes.

To get there we strolled along a street called Peru and crossed other streets, the names of which reminded Eva of her adventures and the countries she had been to: Mexico, Venezuela, Chile, Estados Unidos and Cochabamba which was named after a city high in the Bolivian Andes. She had been everywhere and as we walked, we chatted about her experiences. I was **all ears** because, while she was ending her Latin American adventure, I was just beginning mine and I needed all the advice I could get.

Argentina was in the grip of a brutal military dictatorship at the time but that didn't worry us as we strolled along. We felt perfectly safe. What concerned us more was the cold. Winter was coming and the air was chilly. We couldn't wait to get inside somewhere warm, so we went into the first bar that we came to.

When we entered there was a group of about a dozen old men crowded around a television set at one end of the bar, watching a game of football. The barman and the waiter were absorbed in the game too. The former was standing behind the counter with a great mirror and rows of spirit bottles behind him and the latter leant on the other side as though he was waiting for a drink. Both were watching the game every bit as intently as their customers. At first no one noticed us when we walked in and stood there watching the unfolding drama of the old men and their football match.

Idioms & Short Stories

It must have been a very important game because all their attention was focused on the screen, and they were tensely leaning forward as though to get as close as possible to the action. A moment after we walked in, one of the teams had a shot on goal and half of the men leapt out of their seats cheering loudly with their arms stretched out in triumph.

But they cheered too soon. The ball hit a defender and ricocheted off him and over the goal line. Their cheers turned to groans of agony and they sat down again. The other six men in the group breathed sighs of relief. But the crisis was not yet over. The corner kick was still to come and as the players bunched together in front of the goal, the fans settled down in their seats again leaning forward and staring at the television. Each one was a bundle of nerves, enduring his own private agony. You could feel the tension in the air as one half of the group was willing the ball to go into the net and the others willing it to be kept out.

The tension among the spectators in the bar was so great that they were all halfway out of their seats at the moment the player kicked the ball which flew high and curved in towards the goal. It **hung in the air** for a moment before coming down into the bunch of players. But before any of the attacking team could take advantage of their position, the big goalkeeper for the defending side punched the ball so hard it flew almost to the halfway mark.

Phew! The tension was released. The teams scrambled downfield and the old men in the bar resumed their seats.

It was then that we were noticed. First the barman noticed us and came over to show us to a table. The movement attracted the attention of the old football fans who turned to stare at us as we sat down. But they only stared for a moment or two. Suddenly the crowd at the football roared loudly as there was another attacking move and the old men swung their attention back to the TV and resumed their hunched, tense positions waiting for the explosion of joy or agony that would come if a goal was scored.

We sat down and ordered our meal from the waiter who kept looking over his shoulder at the television. He could not hide the fact that he was more interested in the **ebb and flow** of the match than he was in what we were going to have for dinner.

But we made it easy for him. We both settled for the Argentine classic of steak, salad and chips, or fries as Eva had learned to call them in the United States. To drink, we had a carafe of wine and some soda water. While we waited, we chatted, and she gave me plenty of good tips and advice about where to go and what to see in South America. She had been just about everywhere!

While we chatted, **out of the corner of my eye**, I **couldn't help but** notice that a couple of the old men – one with a long, shaggy, white beard and the other wearing an old baseball cap – kept dragging their gaze away from the screen and looking at us. Or should I say looking at Eva? It certainly wasn't me that was distracting their attention from the big match. I'm sure Eva must have noticed it, just as I had, but we ignored them and focused on our splendid meal.

Although this was simple food, the meal was fit for a king. It was cooked to perfection, and it **lived up to** Argentina's well-deserved reputation for having the best steak in the whole world.

"An old friend of mine came from Argentina," said Eva, "and she told me that Argentina never changes. The politics are always terrible, and the food is always brilliant."

"Well, your friend wasn't wrong," I **couldn't help but** agree.

In the background, the match ebbed and flowed, the advantage went **back and forth**. First one side got the upper hand, and then the other. And each time the advantage moved from one to the other, half of the old men would jump to their feet with loud cheers and shouts while the rest would sink into their chairs with groans of anguish.

They were becoming steadily more excited. Whenever one group cheered with joy, the other hung its head in dismay. And they **took turns** to abuse the referee, **calling him all the names under the sun**. They reached extremes of **agony and ecstasy** when first one side and then the other scored a goal. At moments like these they forgot all about the strangers in the bar. But when the tension eased their attention began to wander and the old man in the baseball cap kept glancing back over his shoulders at us.

The game ended just as we were finishing our meal. The score was one-all, a draw. We had shared a dessert and were having coffee when **nature called**. I had drunk the **lion's share** of the wine and had to go to the toilet.

While I was in there, I heard an almighty crash, the sound of breaking glass and a shout followed by more shouting. Someone in the kitchen must have dropped something, I

A date to remember

thought, and boy, were they **making a big song and dance** about it.

I washed my hands and when I emerged into the bar was shocked to realize that I had **jumped to the wrong conclusion**. The noise had not come from someone dropping something in the kitchen but from an all-in brawl among the old men. Despite their great age they fought each other as though they were in a Wild West movie. Punches were thrown, glasses were smashed, and chairs flew through the air.

What had happened was obvious. Neither set of fans would accept that the draw was a just result, each thought that their team should have won and the discussion had rapidly escalated into an argument and from there into outright physical violence.

The barman looked very worried, and he came over to Eva and me and said we should get out of there **quick smart**. He had called the police and it would be a good idea for us if we were not there when they arrived.

Such was the political climate of the times we did not need any more encouragement. The last thing we wanted was to get tangled up with the police force of a brutal military dictatorship. We had heard stories about what could happen to innocent people at their hands. And, in any case, Eva had a plane to catch the next day.

So, we hastily paid the bill, put on our coats and **high-tailed it** down the dark, chilly streets to the sounds of distant police sirens drawing ever closer, retracing our steps along Peru and across all those other reminders of Eva's grand tour of the

Americas: Cochabamba, Estados Unidos, Chile, Venezuela and Mexico.

I never did find out what happened to the aged brawlers in the bar. I didn't dare ask anyone and never went back. I assumed they were all hauled off for a night in the cells and then told to try to behave like adults and stop being a public nuisance.

However, I did discover the true reason for the brawl, which was not, as I had assumed, the result of the football match. When Eva and I caught our breath, I commented how ridiculous it was for grown men to be fighting like children over the outcome of a game.

"They're a bunch of sore losers," I concluded.

I was being very somber and serious, indicating to Eva that I did not approve of violence, and I fully expected that she would agree with me and share my disdain for these old grandfathers who were setting such a poor example of sportsmanship. But Eva just laughed and told me I shouldn't be so quick to **jump to conclusions**. The true cause of the brawl wasn't the football game, it was her.

As had been obvious from the moment we had been noticed, the old men had been deeply impressed by her presence and when the game ended, the old man in the baseball cap had **plucked up the courage** to approach Eva and had offered to buy her a drink. This had seemed to provoke a surge of jealousy in the old man with the shaggy beard.

The two old men had engaged in a shouting match right in front of her over who would have the privilege of buying the attractive young woman a drink. She never even got the opportunity to say "yes, please" or "no, thank you". The argument had become so heated that suddenly the man in the cap threw a punch at the man with the white beard.

That punch started the general brawl and pretty soon glasses, crockery and chairs were flying through the air and old men were rolling around on the floor trying to do as much harm to each other with their fists as they could. Even the sudden sharp crash of the chair smashing into the mirror behind the bar had no effect on the brawlers.

If there was one consolation in all the drama, it was that Eva herself remained untouched by the violence swirling around her. She stayed right where she was, looking startled but still a picture of calm in the **eye of the storm**. Despite their anger, passion and aggression, the old men were sure not to lay a finger on her. In that respect at least, they remained gentlemen to the very end.

First steps

Fill in the gaps in sentences (1)-(22) with the appropriate idioms from the list below.

(1) She never says it directly, but you ... that she does not **get on** with her co-star.

(2) I was ... as she told me about what happened at the office Christmas party when a couple of our colleagues got drunk and tried to throw the CEO in the river.

(3) When my friends asked me to look after their place for them while they went away on holiday, I was ... because they lived in a fantastic apartment with fabulous view and just a few steps from the beach.

(4) Your mistake could cost the company a lot of money and you'll be in big trouble if the boss finds out. But, if you fix it … maybe no one will have time to notice.

(5) After robbing the bank, Bonnie and Clyde, … in a stolen car.

(6) They had known each other for a few months before they decided to …. They went to see a show and afterwards went for drinks at a cosy little bar near the theatre. It was a great success and they have been going out together ever since.

(7) The new mobile phone … all the hype. It was much better than all the others.

(8) Great basketballers, such as LeBron James and Michael Jordan, sometimes seem to … as the leap to make a slam dunk.

(9) Floods had destroyed the bridge, so we had to spend all day going … over the river in a boat to bring enough supplies to keep the town going until the bridge could be replaced.

(10) The shop was very busy, and he was serving a customer when he noticed … that a boy had taken a chocolate bar off the counter and slipped it into his pocket.

(11) Learning a new language can be …: Agony because it is sometimes very hard, almost painful, to **come to grips with** the grammar and vocabulary but ecstasy because it is a very special pleasure when you can read, write, speak and listen in your new language.

(12) The young football player was a … when he arrived at the stadium where he would play for his country for the first time.

A date to remember

(13) When the police found the dead body, they assumed it was a case of murder but **it turned out** to be …. The old man had died of natural causes.

(14) He drank three glasses of wine before going to see the movie which was a big mistake because … and he missed the climax when he had to go to the bathroom.

(15) The decision to spend billions of dollars on a new stadium was hugely controversial, with many people arguing the money should be spent on improving the city's crumbling infrastructure. As the public official most responsible for the decision, the mayor was right ….

(16) When the government proposed a law they did not like, the activists … about it, mounting protests, waving placards and blocking roads.

(17) When two cars collided at the intersection near my house the other day, one driver was swearing and cursing at the other one. He called him ….

(18) He was very shy, so it took a great effort for him to … to ask her out on a date.

(19) The old couples' lives were regulated by the … of the tide. When the tide ebbed, they would stroll along the wide sandy beach. But when it flowed, it came right up to the seawall, and they had to walk along the road.

(20) The children … to play with the toy fire engine. First, George had a turn and then Nancy.

(21) The teenager boy was always hungry and whenever there was food on the table he always ate the …, leaving very little for anyone else.

(22) He was advised to … of the opportunity to improve his skills.

A. Took turns
B. lion's share
C. pluck up the courage
D. lived up to
E. go out on a date
F. get the impression
G. it was nothing of the kind
H. only too happy to oblige
I. all ears
J. hang in the air
K. ebb and flow
L. out of the corner of his eye
M. back and forth
N. all the names under the sun
O. agony and ecstasy
P. nature called
Q. made a big song and dance
R. quick smart
S. high-tailed it
T. bundle of nerves
U. in the eye of the storm
V. take advantage of

The one true thing

Have you ever noticed that no matter which queue you join at the supermarket **checkout**, it's always the slowest? This is, in essence, the law of queues. It explains everything **in a nutshell**. If you have never noticed it, let me explain exactly how it works with a story about what happened the last time I did the shopping.

My **shopping list** included some fresh fruit and vegetables, meat, fish, some canned food such as beans. Eggs, of course, and bread plus tea, coffee beans and milk. And dishwashing liquid too. We had just about **run out of** dishwashing liquid.

It was a Saturday morning in summer and stepping from the warm outdoors into the cool supermarket was like going from a hot oven into a crowded refrigerator. It seemed like the whole town was there doing their weekly grocery shopping and the low temperature could not calm the **frayed nerves**, irritation and frustration as people tried to get the chore done as quickly as possible. But the **checkouts** acted as **speed bumps**, slowing them all down. Long queues clogged every single one and the standard supermarket muzak was punctuated by a chorus of beep-beep-beeping at the tills.

It did not take long to fill my trolley and I **sized up** the queues at the **checkout**, trying to calculate which one would get me out of there quickest. **As it turned out**, the shortest queue was the one closest to the supermarket entrance. The ones at the other end were the longest as people finished their shopping and headed for the nearest **checkout** with their trollies overflowing. I wasn't going to be caught like that. I doubled back to the short queue where I was third in line, whereas the other queues had four, five or even six people waiting.

Things went very smoothly at first. Beep, beep, beep went the **checkout** scanner as the groceries of the woman at the head of our queue were totalled up. Smooth and efficient it was, until she came to pay. That's when the trouble started. I could never figure out exactly what the problem was – either her card was faulty or there wasn't enough money in her account or maybe something else – but whatever it was, it held us up while the supervisor was called and there was a long discussion.

We were stalled and we could hear the beep, beep, beeping that told us that all the people at the other **checkouts** were going through, if not as quickly as they would like, then at a steady pace while we were stuck. In front of me were an elderly couple. He manned the front of the trolley and was unloading while she stood at the rear holding her purse, ready to pay when the time came.

She smiled at me reassuringly, a picture of saintly patience. She certainly wasn't letting the delay get to her and I wanted to show her that I didn't mind either so **in jest** I **rolled my eyes** and said, "It's the law of queues."

"The law of what?" she replied, looking puzzled rather than amused.

"The law of queues," I explained. "It states that no matter which queue you join, it's always the slowest."

"Really?" She responded with an air of mildly patronising, questioning, scepticism. She had taken me seriously even though I had been joking as a way of easing the tension.

"Yes," I said and pointed to a woman in a blue top, sailing out of the supermarket with her laden trolley while we were still stuck in line. I pointed out that just a few moments before she had been second in line in the queue next to us and while we remained where we were, she was on her way home.

To me this was proof that the law of queues was operating as it should. If I couldn't make the nice old lady smile, at least I could prove my point! But the old lady seemed unconvinced. She didn't say anything just gave me another patronising look.

Clearly, I was compelled to drive home my advantage and make her see, so I delivered my punch line: "It's the one true thing in the universe," I declared smugly.

"Young man," she replied with a saintly smile, "Jesus Christ is the one true thing in the universe."

I was so embarrassed that I turned red. I could feel the burning sensation on my face. It was **game, set and match** to her. I didn't know what to say and, fortunately, I didn't need to reply because just then the difficulties at the head of our queue were resolved – I don't know how having been distracted by our discussion – and the beep, beep, beeping had resumed.

The one true thing

Once things were moving again, the old couple passed smoothly through the **checkout**. And then it was my turn. I unloaded my groceries but before anything of mine could be beeped through, a new **checkout** operator arrived to take over and there was a short delay as she changed the tills and logged on to the system.

The delay was not too long though and soon the beep, beep, beeping was **under way** again and this time it was my stuff going through. Beep went the packaged noodles, beep went the dried soups, beep, beep went the cans of tuna. It was all going so smoothly. Beep went the potatoes and lettuce. Beep, beep, beep went the milk, eggs and bread.

Perhaps I had overdone it a bit, maybe the law of queues wasn't really the one true thing in the universe, after all. Beep, beep, beep went the sardines, baked beans, salt and pepper. Maybe the law of queues was just one of the many true things, I thought. Beep, beep went the tea and coffee beans. But maybe not. Maybe it wasn't even that. Maybe it wasn't true at all but just the **irrational obsession** of an impatient, bad tempered and irascible man. Maybe the old lady was right, it didn't really make any sense at all.

I was almost there, almost finished and it seemed that, for the first time in history, the law of queues had failed to predict the future. Reluctantly, I had to concede defeat, to myself at least. The little old lady had long gone and no one else there could possibly understand.

But there was one last item moving forward on the conveyor belt: the dishwashing liquid. The **checkout** operator reached for it and tilted it when looking for the bar code. That one small gesture changed everything. The cap came off and dishwashing liquid spilled out over the counter, the scanner and some of my groceries which were still waiting to be packed.

The operator immediately punched her bell for assistance and the sharp ring cut right across the beeping chorus and the muzak. Within seconds the supervisor and a couple of helpers appeared with buckets and mops and sponges and cloths. They were all efficiency and apologies as they set about cleaning up the mess.

But efficient as they were, they could not conceal the fact that my shopping was now stalled one beep short of completion while in every other aisle the **checkouts** were beeping away as if they were happy cicadas in summer and people, who had joined their lengthy queues long after I had joined my short one, were completing the great chore of Saturday morning shopping and heading off to enjoy their weekend.

Just then I looked up and saw, through the big plate glass windows at the front of the supermarket, the little old couple driving out of the car park.

"Yes," I said under my breath, "the one true thing in the universe."

The teller heard but didn't quite catch what I had said. "What was that," she asked.

"Oh, never mind," I replied.

First steps

Fill in the gaps in sentences (1)-(10) with the appropriate idioms from the list below.

The one true thing

(1) …, he started a petition to have all teachers banned from the campus for a week. Although it was just a joke, some teachers did not find it funny.

(2) The coach … the other football team and decided that all-out attack was the way his men would win the game.

(3) The protesters had been blocking the road for hours and the motorists who were stuck in traffic were showing signs of …. They got out of their cars and shouted at the protesters, and some even grabbed them and tried to drag them off the road.

(4) Hardly anyone ever stuck to the speed limit near our house, so the council installed … on the road to force them to slow down. It worked very well because motorists knew they would damage their cars and possibly injure themselves as well if they drove fast into one of those bumps.

(5) When he told her how sorry he was, she just …. She had heard it all before. He was always sorry when caught out but that never stopped him doing it again.

(6) One of the most famous, and longest, novels in the English language is *Ulysses* by James Joyce. It is 700 pages and very difficult to summarise. But …, it is set in Dublin and tells the story of a day in the life of Leopold Bloom and his friends and acquaintances.

(7) It is fair enough to criticise politicians and dislike them, but our neighbour's dislike of the local mayor became an …. The mayor and all his shortcomings were just about the only topic he ever talked about.

(8) Smith demonstrated that Jones had got his facts and figures wrong on a number of key issues. At that point, it was … to Smith, there was no question that he had won the debate.

Idioms & Short Stories

(9) Our pantry cupboard was nearly empty, so we had a long ... when we went to the supermarket. We needed everything from food to toiletries and domestic cleaning products. By the time we had finished our shopping we had just about everything on the list: fresh fruit and vegetables, meat, tea and coffee, pasta and rice, bread, toothpaste, milk and food for the cat as well.

(10) Trials are ... for a new drug which, it is hoped, will slow down the ageing process.

A. in a nutshell
B. shopping list
C. frayed nerves
D. speed bumps
E. sized up
F. In jest
G. rolled her eyes
H. game, set and match
I. under way
J. irrational obsession

Glossary

a bird in the hand is worth two in the bush
This expression means that it is better to take what you can now, rather than wait in the expectation of getting more later. The former is certain, the latter uncertain. Variations of this expression exist in many languages; the important thing is to recognise that the same idea that lies behind them all.

above board
An expression that means legal, legitimate and out in the open. It is believed to be derived from card games in which players who put their hands under the table (or under the board) were suspected of switching their cards. Hence, to be **above board** is to be open and honest and clearly not cheating or doing anything against the rules.

agony and ecstasy
This expression comes from the title of a historical novel, *The Agony and the Ecstasy*, about the life of the great Renaissance

painter Michelangelo Buonarotti. The title reflects the pain, on the one hand, and the deep happiness, on the other, that he experienced in his life. The title, if not the book, made such a deep impression on newspaper headline writers that it has become a standard expression to convey the sense that someone has experienced great highs and lows in their lives. It seems especially apt for sports people. **Triumph and disaster** is a similar expression.

all ears
When someone is **all ears**, it means they are paying great attention to what they are being told, especially when what they are being told is gossip. In other words, they are very interested.

approaching middle age
A standard way of saying that someone is nearly middle aged, which can be defined as between the ages of about 45 and 60. Before that, you are young and after that you are old.

as it turned out/it turned out
The result of something, how it ended.

as nice as pie
There are two senses in this phrase. One is that someone is being unexpectedly pleasant or respectful. The other is that they are being excessively so. There are many expressions in English that have the same structure: **as mad as a snake**, **as merry as a cricket**, **as poor as a church mouse**, **as light as a feather**, **as long as your arm** and many, many more.

at the back of my mind

When you are aware of something but are not actively thinking about it, you can say it is **at (or in) the back of your mind**. Often, this expression is used when you are worried or concerned about something but have not specifically identified what it is. You could say, for instance, "I accepted the job offer even though **at the back of my mind** I thought I wasn't the right person to do it".

back and forth

Synonyms include **to and fro, ebb and flow, come and go**.
See **comings and goings, ebb and flow**

been there, done that

A condensed way of saying **I have been there, and I have done that**, in other words, you have the knowledge and experience.

bundle of nerves

A **bundle** is when you have a number of similar things tied together in some way, for example a **bundle** of sticks, when you have a lot or sticks, or a **bundle** of cash, when you have cash. When you are very anxious, jittery or nervous you can say you are a **bundle of nerves**.

Note that with bundles of sticks and cash you use the verb **have** but with nerves use the verb **be**. He **has a bundle of cash** in his back pocket, but he **is a bundle of nerves** because he is worried about his exams.

Glossary

bursting with energy
To have excessive amounts of energy. Young people often **burst with energy**. Old people not so much. You can also **burst with excitement** when you are very excited.

calling him all the names under the sun
Use this expression when you want to say that some swore at someone else but, to avoid offending your listeners or your readers, you do not want to repeat the swear words. If you say "he **called him all the names under the sun**" people will know that he used a lot of swear words that are not usually seen in print or used in polite company.

call it a night
To declare that you have gone as far as you are willing to go and will go no further. As far as you are concerned the matter, whether it is something to do with your job or a social occasion, is over and done with, the night is complete. You say **call it a day** if what you are referring to has taken place during the day.

caught his eye
When something catches your eye, it attracts your attention in some way. You could say "the painting **caught my eye** because the colours were so bright". You can use the same expression when you are trying to attract attention to yourself. For instance, "I am trying to **catch the waiter's eye** because I want to order more wine". The adjectival form is **eye-catching**, which you use to describe something that attracts attention. For example, "she wore an **eye-catching** multi-coloured jacket".

came of age/come of age
To reach the age of adulthood. In the old days it used to be 21 but in many, if not most, countries it is now 18.

catch up
To meet someone who you haven't seen for a while to exchange news and chat about things that interest you both. Can be for business or pleasure. But note that **catch up** can also mean to follow someone and finally reach them. For instance, "in the end, the police **caught up** with the fleeing bank robbers" or, in a race, you could say "the runner was in second place for most of the race, but he **caught up** to the leader just before the finish line". It can also mean to finish work that is incomplete or overdue. For instance, "I can't go out tonight because I have to **catch up** on my homework." **Caught up** can also mean to be entangled in something, either and emotion or a scandal. For example, "wasn't he the one **caught up** in that corruption scandal?"

changed his tune
Despite appearances, this expression has nothing to do with music. People **change their tune** when they change their account or story. "She told the police her partner could not have robbed the bank because he was with her at the time. But later she **changed her tune** and said that, in fact, she hadn't seen him for days." It can also mean to change your behaviour or attitude: "He used to be rude and difficult to deal with but lately he's **changed his tune**. Now he's polite, friendly and very helpful."

Glossary

cheap knock-off

In many places, you can buy imitations of expensive luxury products such as Rolex watches or Louis Vuitton bags. At first glance, they may look like the real thing, but a closer examination will tell you that they are fake. Another clue is the price. They are always much, much cheaper than the real thing. The expression for something like this is **cheap knock-off**.

check out/checkout

Informally, this means to investigate something. If you received an offer of a new job, you would **check it out** before accepting. Formally, **check out** is to leave a hotel. You **check out** when you pay the bill and leave. Note that as a noun, the **checkout** is the place where the cashier sits in a supermarket and you pay your bill and pack your groceries.

chill in the air

When you talk about a **chill** in reference to the weather, you mean it is cool or cold but not freezing cold. **Chill** is also a synonym for cold, as in when you are sick and have a runny nose and sometimes a fever. You say catch a cold or catch a **chill**.

cold, hard cash

This stock phrase is a way of emphasising or exaggerating the idea that something is being paid by cash rather than by credit card.

For some reason, cash is always cold and hard, never soft or warm.

comings and goings

An idiom used to describe lots of people or things moving in and out of somewhere. For instance, the **comings and goings** of people at the office, or passengers at a train station, or planes at an airport.

The verb form of the expression is **come and go**, people, planes and trains **come and go**. Even fashion **comes and goes** meaning that something that goes out of fashion one year, might come back into fashion years later.

come a cropper/coming a cropper

To suffer a heavy fall or mishap of some kind, not necessarily physical. Origins of this expression are uncertain. Some say it derives from another expression **neck and crop**, which refers to birds, meaning the whole bird, everything. Others, that it refers to a printing machine named a Cropper after its inventor. If you got your fingers stuck in the machine you would suffer a serious injury. Hence, to **come a cropper**.

come to grips with

An idiom that means to confront a problem or to make an effort to overcome a problem or to learn something.

For example: "It took him a while but eventually he **came to grips** with the issue of falling productivity in his company and produced a plan to help everyone improve their performance."

comfortably off

Having enough money to provide for all your needs. Not rich but not poor either, somewhere in between.

Glossary

couldn't help but ...
The standard pattern **couldn't help + but ...** or just **couldn't help ...** is used when you have seen, heard or done something without intention.

could have knocked him down with a feather
An expression applied to someone who is greatly surprised, shocked or stunned. For example: "I always thought they were blissfully happy so when I heard that they were getting divorced, **you could have knocked me down with a feather**".

dropped me off
When someone takes you to your destination and leaves you there, you say they **dropped you off**. It is the opposite of **picked me up** (see below).

drudge work
Work that is routine, boring, hard and often dirty. The opposite would be **glamorous work, exciting work, interesting work**.

easy come, easy go
What you win, gain or earn easily, you can lose just as easily.

ebb and flow
This expression has a literal meaning and a metaphorical one. Literally it refers to the tide, when it goes out, it ebbs and when it comes in, it flows. Metaphorically it can refer to any human activity in which things change or **come and go**. It is

especially useful in the context of sporting contests which **ebb and flow** as first one side, or one player, and then the other has the advantage. But you can also use it to talk about the **ebb and flow** in a discussion, argument or debate or about the **ebb and flow** of the economy among many other things.

See **comings and goings, back and forth**

empty handed

Literally, to have nothing in your hands. To leave **empty handed** is to depart without getting what you came for. It could be used in the context of shopping: "He went to buy a tin of beans, but the shop did not have the variety he liked, and he left **empty handed**". It could also be used in the context of a crime: "The robbers fled **empty handed** when the police arrived".

every now and then

From time to time, occasionally. To help you remember, listen to the chorus of *Total Eclipse of the Heart* a huge hit of the 1980s by Bonnie Tyler http://tinyurl.com/4sjnkrw8 in which **every now and then** is repeated over and over again.

extra-terrestrial beings

The prefix **extra** means outside or beyond and **terrestrial** means to do with the earth.

So, this common phrase is used to refer to any creatures or organisms that might exist outside the earth, on other planets or in other parts of the universe.

Colloquial terms for **extra terrestrials** include **Martians** or **little green men**.

Glossary

eye of the storm

Literally, the centre of a storm where things are often calm and quiet. Metaphorically, to be at the centre of some great conflict or dispute.

false-flag attack

When a military organisation or some other group carries out an attack while making it appear that someone else was responsible.

far too risky

Something that stands a high chance of failure is **risky**. If you say it is **too risky**, you are saying that the chances of failure are so high that you will not try it. If you add **far** and say it is **far too risky** you are saying the dangers and chances of failure are even greater. You can use **far too** with lots of words and ideas: **far too** expensive / high / low / bright / wild / drunk / rich / worried / greedy / aggressive / timid and so on.

fallen well short/fell well short

To **fall short** is to fail. For example, if someone had the ambition of becoming a chef in an expensive restaurant but ended up flipping hamburgers in a fast-food chain, you would say he had **fallen short of** his ambitions.

In this case, as he was nowhere near what he wanted to achieve, you can add emphasis with **well**. He **fell well short** of his goal. You can also say that a company has **fallen short** of its sales targets when it does not sell as much of its product as it had planned .

fool's game

A **fool's game** is any activity or project that is futile and certain to fail. Often used to refer to gambling games because the gambler nearly always loses but also for love when a relationship breaks up. A good way to get the expression into your head, is listen to Bonnie Tyler's *It's a Heartache*, which features it in the chorus: https://tinyurl.com/3dk7ra5f.

You could also say **mug's game**, **mug** being a synonym for fool. See **mug punter**, below.

frayed nerves

Collocation to describe feelings of anxiety or frustration. **Fray** literally means to wear out, as when cloth or material becomes frayed and has lots of loose ends. Metaphorically, it goes with **nerves** to describe what happens when someone is tense, angry, anxious and frustrated. See also **bundle of nerves**.

fruitless day

Despite appearances, this collocation does not mean a day without fruit. Rather, it means a day without success. A synonym would be an **unproductive day** and an antonym a **fruitful day**, although this is much less common. **Fruitless** can be used with any endeavour that fails to produce results. You can have **fruitless** talks, deliberations, wars, conferences, strategies, policies, programs and so on.

game, set and match

A stock phrase that signals the end of a tennis match when one player wins the final game and the final set and therefore the match. It is also used in a metaphorical sense to say that someone has won an argument or dispute even if it has nothing whatsoever to do with tennis.

games of chance
A **game of chance** is any type of game that requires more luck (i.e. chance) than skill. Many gambling games such as dice, roulette and, to an extent, many card games are **games of chance**.

get the impression
When you form an idea or opinion about something even though you do not have enough information. Synonyms could be **think** or **feel**. The opposite would be to state something with certainty. For instance, "I **got the impression** he was going out with her" (an opinion based on insufficient information) as against, "He **was** going out with her" which is a statement of fact.

getting on in years
A gentle way to say ageing or growing old. Usually, people just say **getting on**. You need to watch the context closely here because **get on** can also mean to climb on to something or to enter something. "The old man was **getting on** the bus when he dropped his ticket."

Also, be aware that to **get on well** with someone, or just **get on**, means that you are friendly with them. Often this is used in the negative. You will hear people saying "oh, they don't **get on**" meaning they don't like each other.

give in to

To surrender to someone or something. You could say, for instance: "you should not **give in to** temptation and eat that big ice cream". You could also say, "the government **gave in to** the demands of the protesters". However, when it comes to armies defeated in battle, you should not use **give in to**. Only **surrender** will do in that context: "The army **surrendered** to…"

given up on

To **give up** is to **surrender** and when people do this, we say they have **given up**. To **give up on** something is to stop trying. Sometimes, when things are very bad and people are so depressed that they just don't feel like doing anything anymore, we say they have **given up on** life.

go out on a date

A **date** in this context is a social occasion usually between two people who are either romantically involved or considering a romantic involvement. When you intend to meet someone for a date you say you are **going out on a date**. If you are in a relationship with someone but are not engaged or married, you say you are **going out with them** or **going steady** with them or **dating** them.

got the hang of it

An idiom of unknown origin which means to learn how to do something or to acquire a skill. For instance: "When I first tried to ride a bike I kept falling off. But after a while I **got the hang of it** and I haven't fallen off since."

Glossary

grasp the full extent of

To fully understand or to understand completely. Literally, **grasp** is to take hold of something in your hand but in this context, it means to understand something, to take hold of the meaning. The **full extent** literally means the full distance or the full area but, in this context, the sense is the **full meaning**.

great minds think alike

When two people say the same thing at the same time they often add this expression. Never do you hear them say "dull minds think alike" even though that would usually be more apt.

gritted teeth

To **grit your teeth** is to close your mouth tightly, especially when you are angry or determined. If someone speaks while their teeth are gritted, we say they spoke through **gritted teeth**.

had a dip

Dip as a verb means to put something briefly into a liquid. For instance, you can **dip** bread into oil or a sauce. However, in this prefabricated expression, **dip** is used as a noun to mean a short swim. So, you can say I **had a dip** in the sea, or I **went for a dip** in the river.

hail-fellow-well-met

This compound adjective is used to describe someone who is easy going, friendly or good company. It can be used negatively or positively. *Brewer's Dictionary of Phrase and Fable* says it often has a negative sense, that is someone who is so friendly and cheerful that they are annoying but, in my opinion, it is usually used in a positive sense.

hanging out for

If you are very thirsty or hungry and waiting for your dinner, you can say you are **hanging out for** food or drink.

If you happen to be a smoker, you can also say you are **hanging out for** a cigarette if you haven't had one for a while. But note that **hanging out** by itself means something quite different: to spend time with friends.

high hopes

A collocation which means that you are very optimistic about achieving your goals.

A good way to remember the phrase and its meaning is to listen to the song *High Hopes* which was a big hit back in the early 1960s. Originally performed by Frank Sinatra, it was part of the soundtrack of a film, *A Hole in the Head*, and won an Oscar as best original song in 1960. A version with the lyrics can be found at: http://tinyurl.com/2p9w5jnj

high-tailed it

To escape, run away. Originally a Canadian phrase referring to horses which always held their tails in the air as they fled or stampeded.

You could say the bank robbers **high-tailed it** down the high street with all the loot when they heard the police sirens in the distance.

Glossary

honoured in the breach

This idiom is a quotation from Shakespeare and in the twenty-first century, it is used to refer to a rule or law that is rarely obeyed. We say it is "more **honoured in the breach** than the observance." In other words, the rule is more often broken than followed.

However, the original meaning, in *Hamlet*, was that it was better to break bad customs or habits rather than keep them. Hamlet, the Prince of Denmark, is referring to the King's custom of carousing late at night. Hamlet does not approve and says, "To my mind … it is a custom more **honoured in the breach** than the observance," and goes on to complain that other nations will take the Danes for drunkards because of the King's conduct.

hung in the air

A prefabricated phrase to express what happens when something is stationary in the air, a balloon for instance. More often it is used for something that appears for a moment to be stationary in the air and unsupported, even though it is really moving. Sometime basketballers appear to **hang in the air** when they go for a shot. You can also use this phrase to describe something that is unsaid: "The question that **hung in the air** was who would pay for the damage".

if I were you

A way of giving advice to someone. It forms the following pattern **if I were you + I would ….** For instance: "**If I were you, I'd study computers**."

in a nutshell
Summarised very briefly, so brief that it could fit in the shell of a nut. For example, "It was a long report but, **in a nutshell**, the project was far too expensive and not likely to be profitable.

in jest
Joking, jokingly. **Jest** is an old-fashioned word for **joke**, in the middle ages comedians were called **jesters**.

irrational obsession
An **obsession** is a feeling or idea that dominates all of one's thoughts. It is often paired with the adjective **irrational** to intensify the meaning. However, this is not strictly necessary because an **obsession** is, by definition, **irrational**. Yet native speakers nearly always use the two words together.

in the long run
An idiom that means **over a long period of time**. It derives from the idea of a long-distance run and is often used to describe a theatrical work or some sort of exhibition that is very popular and therefore lasts for a long time or, in other words, has a **long run**. The antonym is **short run**.

in the middle of the field
This stock phrase refers to the position of a competitor in a race. The competitor could be a person, a team or a horse. If you are **in the middle of the field** you are about halfway between the leader and the competitor in last place.

Glossary

I told you so
If you warn someone against doing something and they do it anyway and then suffer the predicted consequences, you can say **I told you so** which is a way of reminding them that you had warned them. But be careful, the last thing people who have **come a cropper** want to hear is someone saying **I told you so**. It sounds arrogant and condescending and is a good way to lose friends and make enemies.

jump to conclusions / jumped to the conclusion
When someone makes a decision before examining the evidence or thinking about it very much you can say they **jumped to the (or a) conclusion**.

kill time
To find things to do to keep yourself occupied and prevent boredom when you have lots of spare time. For instance, you might say "I was early for my appointment, so to **kill time** I went and had a cup of coffee".

last throw of the dice
Last chance or last opportunity. The expression refers to dice, a game of chance in which a player throws the dice to see what numbers come up.

learning the ropes
This idiom means to learn the routines and details of a new job or task. It comes from the days of sailing ships when the

crew needed a thorough knowledge of all the ropes in the rigging to be able to do their jobs properly.

lion's share
The greatest part of something. The expression comes from one of Aesop's fables in which a group of animals team up to hunt for their dinner but, after the kill is made, the lion claims all of the meat for himself. The expression can be used in a positive sense. "He did the **lion's share** of the work," means he did most of the work.

lived up to
You can use this expression to refer to people or things. Something or someone that **lives up to** expectations or **lives up to** its reputation, has turned out to be as expected or as hoped. For example, you could say "we had a marvellous time on holiday. The hotel **lived up to** expectations". Or "we had heard good things about her, and she **lived up to** her reputation." Related expressions are **live it down** and **live it up**. The former means to continue living in such a way as to make people forget something bad or embarrassing that you have done. The latter means to celebrate wildly.

long odds
In horse racing the **odds** are what bookmakers (the people who take bets) offer to punters (the people who make bets) betting on horses. The horses deemed most likely to win a race are on **short odds** say, for example 5/2. This means that for every $2 you bet, you stand to gain $5 plus your original $2 if

Glossary

your horse wins. But if your horse is thought highly unlikely to win, it will be at **long odds**, say 100/1. This means that if your horse (known as a **long shot**) does win the race against all expectations, you get $101, the $100 in winnings plus your original stake of $1. The expressions **long odds** and **short odds** can be used metaphorically in other contexts as well to express the likelihood or unlikelihood of something occurring.

long time, no see

This is a condensed way of saying "It's a long time since I've seen you" or "it's a long time since we've seen each other". The expression is said to be derived from a Chinese phrase with a similar meaning and is in widespread use on both side of the Atlantic.

It is well worth remembering because, according to Eric Partridge, author of *A Dictionary of Slang and Unconventional English*, it is (or was) perhaps the most widely used catch phrase in the world.

makes a big fuss of them

To **make a fuss of someone** is to pay them a lot of attention, so to **make a big fuss of someone** is to make them feel like they're the star of the show.

But to **make a big fuss about something** is quite different, it means to **complain loudly**. For example, "the passenger **made a big fuss about the food** on the plane. Apparently, it was not up to his usual standards." See also **making a big song and dance** (below).

making a big song and dance
This has nothing to do with dancing or singing. Rather it refers to complaining loudly, excessively or unnecessarily about something. Similar expressions include **make a big fuss about something** (see above), **kick up a fuss** and **much ado about nothing**, which is the title of a Shakespeare play.

man of the world
One who is sophisticated, knowledgeable and experienced. The opposite of someone who is naïve, inexperienced or innocent.

meat and drink
An idiom which is used to indicate that a particular task is both easy and pleasurable. It also has the sense that, while the task may be easy and pleasurable for some people – say those who have the skill and know what they are doing – for others it may be the opposite, difficult and unpleasant. For instance, "Running a mile was **meat and drink** for the fit young athlete, but for his middle-aged father it was pure agony".

milling around
Use this phrase to describe groups of people talking among themselves and moving around usually while waiting for an event to start or something to happen.

mixed feelings
When you feel two or more contradictory emotions about something you can say you have mixed feelings. For instance,

Glossary

if you are offered a much higher salary but to do a job you don't really like, you might say you have **mixed feelings** about it. On the one hand you would like the extra money, but on the other hand you don't want to do the work. You can have mixed feelings about anything: books, films, movies, places etc. Having **mixed feelings** is usually a sign of being **undecided**, **uncertain** or **unsure** which are some of the many synonyms you could use instead.

mod cons

Short for **modern conveniences**. In other words, domestic appliances such as fridges, TVs, or any gadgets around the home. Usually appears in the expression **all the mod cons**, meaning something, usually a kitchen, has all the up-to-date equipment.

mug punter

Among other things, **mug** means gullible or easily deceived and **punter** is one who gambles or an ordinary person. So, a **mug punter** is a gullible gambler or person. However, both of these words have numerous other meanings, both formal and idiomatic.

For instance, as a noun **mug** can refer to a large cup for drinking tea and coffee or it can mean a face. As a verb it can mean to rob someone or to study hard for an exam. A **punt** can be a bet, a type of kick in football or a flat-bottomed boat which is propelled by someone with a long pole. So, a **punter** can be one who places the bet, kicks the football or propels the boat. The context will tell you which meaning is intended.

nature called
A euphemism that means someone had to go to the bathroom which is another euphemism for urinate which is a formal word for **piss**, **take a piss**, **have a slash** and so on. But note, **take the piss** means to mock someone or something.

new kid on the block
Kid is the slang word for child in English and **on the block** is a stock phrase meaning in the locality or neighborhood. So, literally this refers to a child who has just moved into a locality or neighborhood. However, it is more commonly used for anyone who has just joined a team or has just started a new job, even though they might not be kids anymore.

night and day
All the time, always. To get a good sense of the meaning listen to the song *Night and Day* performed by Tony Bennet and Lady Gaga: http://tinyurl.com/zxxtuxeu

night out
Collocation meaning an evening of entertainment, it might be a dinner date, a few drinks in a bar with friends, going to the theatre or a club

none the wiser
When you hear or read something, but you learn nothing. For instance: The politician made a long statement but left us **none the wiser** about the government's intentions. In other

words, the politician talked a lot but didn't really reveal anything.

no skin off my nose
You can use this idiom when you want to express the idea that something has not had, or will not have, bad effects on you. The origins are not clear, but one theory is that it comes from the sport of boxing in which a fighter might declare that there is **no skin of my nose** meaning that, despite appearances, he has not been injured by his opponent.

not really my cup of tea
This expression has nothing to do with drinking tea. Rather it is a way of saying that you don't like something or someone or are not interested in them. "He was **not my cup of tea**," means at worst you don't like him and at best you don't have anything in common with him. You could also say "golf is **not my cup of tea**" which means you don't like playing golf.

nothing ever came of it
To come of it means to result from. It is commonly used in this pattern which means at no time did anything result from a particular idea, proposal, policy or plan. "They intended to build a new bridge across the river, but **nothing ever came of their plan**."

nothing of the kind
It was **nothing of the kind** stresses that the thing is question was not at all like what had been assumed.

not uncommon

The meaning of this double-negative lies between common and uncommon. The former being usual or normal and the latter being rare or unusual.

There are many expressions like this in English which use a double negative to express a positive meaning that lies between two extremes: **usual / not unusual / unusual, frequent / not infrequent / infrequent, scientific / not unscientific / unscientific, known / not unknown / unknown**.

The song *It's Not Unusual*, by Welsh singer Tom Jones, which was a huge hit in 1965, is good for practice. You'll find it on You Tube: http://tinyurl.com/bdhjcnem

one more for the road

One last drink before you leave a party or a bar. This expression features in a famous Frank Sinatra song *One for my baby and one more for the road*. You will find it on You Tube http://tinyurl.com/yc2z785s

only too happy to oblige

A slightly humorous way of saying that you are willing to help or to take part in something.

Similar expressions are **only too happy to help** and **only too happy to be of assistance**.

op-shop or thrift shop

Short for **opportunity shop** which is a type of shop that sells second-hand goods to raise money for charity. In the United States they are known as **thrift shops**.

Glossary

out of earshot

An idiom that means too far away to hear something. You can stress it by adding **well** – **well out of earshot** means **far too far** away to hear something. The opposite is **within earshot**, meaning close enough to hear. For example, "The little boy did not come home when his mother called him because he was down at the beach, **well out of earshot**".

out of the corner of my eye

When you see or notice something without looking at it directly, you say **out of the corner of my eye**.

pick me up/pick them up

This idiom has a number of meanings. Most commonly used as a verb, it means to collect someone and take them somewhere. Parents **pick up** their children from school, your friends can come to **pick you up** to take you to the beach. The opposite is to **drop someone off**: parents **drop their children off** at school in the morning, your friends might **drop you off** at home after your day at the beach. (See **dropped me off**, above) Context is important because you can also say "he **picked up** the litter that was on the floor" or "my friend Joe was **picked up** by the police for drunk-driving last night". It can also mean to learn something, especially a language. It is often said that children **pick up** languages much more easily than adults. And a **pick-me-up** is a type of drink that you take to make you feel better, especially when you have a hangover. But this expression is quite old fashioned.

pisses him off/pissed off

To **piss someone off** is to annoy them or make them angry. Hence, **pissed off**, to be annoyed.

It is a swear word and although it is quite common and acceptable in some contexts, in others it might be considered grossly offensive, so it is best not to use it. Note **piss off** is a very rude way of telling someone to go away and leave you alone.

See also, **nature called** (above).

playing for time/played for time

Stock phrase meaning to delay while you decide what to do next.

plucked up the courage/pluck up courage

To get or find the courage to do something dangerous or risky. Synonyms include to **summon up the courage**, to **screw up the courage** or to **steel yourself**.

pop the corks/popped the corks

Open a bottle of Champagne. **Pop the corks** because it makes a popping sound when the cork comes out.

pot of gold at the end of the rainbow

An old legend says that anyone who digs at the end of a rainbow will find a pot of gold buried there.

The expression therefore refers to something that is impossible to obtain or achieve. You will often hear the expressions shortened to just **pot of gold**.

Glossary

professional couple

Collocation meaning two people in a relationship who are white-collar workers or professionals of one sort or another as opposed to people who do manual labour or outdoor jobs.

They might be office workers, lawyers, doctors, government officials and so on. The phrase is common in real estate advertisements which state that a property would be "suitable for a **professional couple**".

put our town on the map

To put something or someone **on the map** is to draw attention to them and make them well-known or even famous.

putting all your eggs into one basket

Investing all your money in one company or one type of investment.

A very risky and foolish strategy because if you drop the basket, you lose everything.

putting a packet on it

To bet a lot of money. It is possibly a reference to your **pay packet**. Nowadays, people are paid by direct transfer or credit, but in the old days workers received their pay in cash and it came in an envelope or **packet**.

quick smart

A collocation to stress that something is done quickly and without delay.

quit while they were ahead

A common piece of advice which gamblers nearly always ignore. It means stop while you are winning, the implication being that if you keep going you will certainly lose. It is often used in other contexts as well. For instance, sports people might decide to quite while they are ahead, meaning that they retire before they get too old.

ran out of/ run out of

This means that all the supplies of something have been exhausted or used up: a car **runs out of** petrol, for instance. During the Covid pandemic it was not unusual for supermarkets to **run out of** flour and toilet paper. You can also say the **petrol ran out** or the **flour had run out**. But note that **run out onto** means something quite different: "The team **ran out onto** the field, ready to play the game of their lives" and "The woman reacted quickly, when the little boy **ran out onto** the road".

receding hairline

What happens when men start to lose the hair along the top of their forehead. We say the **hairline recedes** or the **hairline is receding** hence **receding hairline**.

rolled my eyes/rolled her eyes

A form of body language in which you express annoyance or contempt by turning your eyes upward. Can also be done with humour or irony.

Glossary

scared out of their wits
To be **scared out of your wits** is to be very, very frightened. So frightened that you lose your ability to think or reason, hence **out of your wits**. A good synonym is **terrified**.

scrolling through
A multi-word verb that means the same as **browse** in the context of a computer or smartphone. When you have your mobile device in your hand and you are briefly checking lots of different items on your social media pages, you are **scrolling through** your social media accounts, an action usually performed with your thumb.

second thoughts
To have **second thoughts** is to **change your mind** about something. Another way of putting it is to **think again**.

shopping list
Stock phrase for the note you take to the supermarket to remind you of all the things you need to buy.

shouting a round of drinks
In Australian and New Zealand slang, **shout** as a verb means to buy a round of drinks at the bar and **shout** as a noun is the act of buying drinks. So, someone might say, "I'll **shout** you a beer" which means "I'll buy you a beer". Or someone might say "it's your **shout**, mate" which means it's your turn to buy a beer. This usage is said to date from the days when you had to

shout to the bar staff to get their attention. These days, though, **shout** is also used in contexts other than buying beer in pubs. For instance, you might **shout** someone tickets to a big football match or, if you are very lucky, someone might **shout** you a trip to Paris in springtime.

showed Whitehead to the door

To direct or take someone to the exit of a room or a building. For instance, after a business meeting or a social occasion at your house, you **show your guests to the door**, or you **show them out**. However, if you say **show someone the door** (without the **to**) the meaning changes radically. To **show someone the door** is to get rid of someone who is not wanted. In a work context it is the same as saying giving someone the sack or firing someone. For example, "He didn't reach his sales targets, so they **showed him the door**." In a social context, it might be to break up with someone. For example, "When we asked after her partner, George, she said she had **shown him the door** and hadn't heard from him in months."

show my ignorance/showed his ignorance

To **show your ignorance** is a stock phrase that means to reveal yourself to be ill-informed about something or just plain stupid. Often this is done by asking a stupid question.

shrug of his shoulders

A **shrug** is when you raise both shoulders together. It can also be a verb: he **shrugged his shoulders**. Doing this is a form of body language that indicates you don't know or don't care

Glossary

about something Sometimes, you just say **shrugged**. **Shrug off** means that you dismiss or reject some bad news, threat or setback.

sized up
Size up is to estimate the size or quality of something or someone.

slung over his shoulder
When you carry something – a rifle, a backpack or a bag – with a strap *over* your shoulder, you say it was **slung over your shoulder**. To carry something *on* your shoulder is to have whatever it is – rifle, box, backpack or even a person – on top of your shoulder and not hanging with a strap.

smartened me up/smarten him up
To **smarten up** is to improve your appearance, especially the way you dress. You can also say **smarten up** your behaviour / attitude / ideas.

spartan digs
A prefabricated phrase meaning a dwelling that is very basic and has no luxuries. **Spartan** is an adjective derived from Sparta, the ancient Greek state where there were no luxuries. **Digs** is an English slang word for a rented room.

speed bumps
Literally, **speed bumps** are low ridges built across roads to force cars to slow down. Metaphorically, they mean something

that slows progress more generally. You can say, for instance, that a company hit **speed bumps** in its expansion plans, causing serious losses.

splitting his sides laughing/split my sides laughing
And idiom that means to laugh a lot. Sometimes when you laugh so much that it hurts.

striking blue eyes
To describe eyes that are especially beautiful, attractive or impressive you use the adjective **striking**. You can say **striking blue eyes** or **striking brown eyes**. You can also use **striking** to refer to someone's appearance generally when you mean there was something very **eye-catching** about them, especially in a positive sense. In verb form, you can use it to explain that something or someone has greatly impressed you.

For instance: "That **strikes** me as a very good idea," or "I was **struck** by how much he had matured in the years since I had last seen him".

stuck to his guns
Originally a naval term in which sailors were commanded to **stick by their guns** even though the battle might be going badly for them. Now it has a more peaceful sense.

When you **stick to your guns**, it means that you hold your position or opinion despite resistance and opposition.

For example, "they told her the idea would never work, but she **stuck to her guns** and was proved right in the end".

Glossary

such as it was

This idiom is used to indicate that the thing referred to was insignificant, unimportant or just not very good. For instance, you might hear someone say, "the summer is over, **such as it was**. It did nothing but rain the whole time".

take advantage of

A prefabricated phrase that means to seize an opportunity from someone or some situation. It can be used in a positive sense. To **take advantage of** a job offer, for instance, is no bad thing. But it can also be used in a negative sense, to **take advantage of** someone else's troubles is not a very nice thing to do. For instance, "he was ruthless and had no hesitation in **taking advantage of** people when they were desperate".

taken for a fool

To **take someone for a fool** is to regard them as being stupid. If you hear someone saying "what do you **take me for**?" What they mean is, they think they are being **taken for a fool**.

thickening waist/waist has thickened

A prefabricated phrase to describe someone who is putting on weight, usually as they get older.

thickly wooded

A stock phrase used to describe a piece of land that has lots of trees on it but not as many as a forest. Nor would it be a jungle which is generally described as dense.

thick-set
Used to describe big people, usually men, who are muscular, solid, burly or stocky as opposed to tall or skinny. Olympic weightlifters are usually thick-set as are many wrestlers and rugby players.

thrown in the towel
An expression that means to surrender or give up. It comes from boxing in which a fighter concedes defeat when his trainer throws a towel into the ring.

to die for
Literally this means to die fighting for a cause. For instance, soldiers die for their country when they are killed in battle. But the idiomatic sense of **to die for** is a way of stressing that something – often food – is very good but you don't really mean that you are willing **to die for** a piece of cake. An important point to note is word order. Used with its literal meaning the phrase comes first: "He died for the cause of freedom". But if you want the idiomatic meaning, the phrase comes last: "The chocolate eclairs were **to die for**".

told him where to go
The expression means that you have told someone to go away or that you are not interested in what they have to offer you. To say it directly to someone's face you would say "you know where you can go" but this is extremely rude and not often used. Although strictly speaking this expression is not swearing it is best to avoid it unless you are very confident.

Glossary

took me under their wing

If someone **takes you under their wing**, they are helping, protecting and guiding you just as a mother hen will take her chicks under her wing to look after them.

took turns

When two or more people alternate at doing something. For instance, you can **take turns** doing a particular task at work. Often people **take turns** doing the chores at home, first one person will wash the dishes and then next day, someone else does it.

trigger happy

A stock phrase used to describe someone who is too eager to fire their gun. It can be used literally, relating to firearms, or metaphorically to describe an overly aggressive person, someone who is too willing to start a dispute.

under no illusions

A stock phrase meaning that someone was given no false hopes or false expectations, that they knew the truth at the beginning and were not deceived.

under way

Moving forward and making progress are synonyms. The phrase originally referred to ships which were said to be **under way** when they were moving. It now applies more generally. You can say, for instance, that the football match got **under way** after a short delay because the referee had forgotten to bring his whistle.

unvarnished truth

This collocation means the whole truth and nothing but the truth. Varnish is, literally, a type of coating that is put on timber furniture to make it look shiny and to preserve it. **Unvarnished truth** in this metaphor, therefore, means that nothing has been done to polish the truth and make it seem better than it really is.

Note that this expression is only used in the negative. You can't say the varnished truth. Well, you could but it would sound odd to most English speakers.

warn off/warning people off

To tell someone to stay away from a place or to stop using something that may be harmful. It can imply a threat. For example, "The neighbours had caused so much trouble that he **warned them off** his property and said that if they came back he would call out his dogs".

wee dram

Prefabricated phrase meaning a small drink. **Wee** is Scottish for small and **dram** signifies a small quantity. **Wee dram** always refers to a glass of Scotch whisky. A synonym is **wee drappie**.

well and truly

Synonyms are **decisively** or **completely**. "The team was **well and truly** beaten" or "his career was **well and truly** over".

Glossary

when it came to
When it comes to is in idiomatic expression that means "on the subject/theme/topic of …" You might say "He was a great mathematician, but **when it came to** geometry, he was not very able."

whole host of
Host is the key word here and, in this expression, it means "a great many". So, if you say a **whole host of** other things, you mean a great many other things or a **whole host of** problems, you mean a lot of problems. One thing to note is that the expression may cause some difficulties because **host** is most commonly used in a completely different sense: someone who looks after guests in some way. For example, someone who invites you to dinner or to a party is your **host** and someone who interviews people on a radio show is also a **host**. As a verb **host** means the action of doing these things. The person who invited you to dinner **hosted** the party and the interviewer **hosted** the radio show. Someone who runs a guest house or a bed and breakfast hotel can also be a **host**.

You can't or shouldn't) judge a book by its cover
To make decisions, especially about people, based solely on appearances or superficial factors. A good piece of music to learn this expression by is Bo Diddley's *You Can't Judge a Book by Looking at the Cover* http://tinyurl.com/bdhtmkfy

Answers

Scary night of lights
(1) D, (2) A, (3) G, (4) J, (5) I, (6) E, (7) F, (8) H, (9) B, (10) C (11) K

The first time
(1) J, (2) B, (3) E, (4) C, (5) F, (6) O, (7) G, (8) H, (9) D, (10) K, (11) L, (12) A, (13) P, (14) M, (15) I, (16) N

A bird in the hand
(1) C, (2) Q, (3) R, (4) D, (5) P, (6) E, (7) G, (8) F, (9) N, (10) H, (11) I, (12) K, (13) A, (14) O, (15) J, (16) M, (17) B, (18)L (19) S

Life's lessons
(1) E, (2) D, (3) C, (4) V, (5) F, (6) G, (7) H, (8) J, (9) B, (10) R, (11) L, (12) T, (13) O, (14) K, (15) M, (16) S, (17) N, (18) A, (19) I, (20) P, (21) Q, (22) U (23) W

Answers

A piece of advice

(1) C, (2) P, (3) H, (4) G, (5) D, (6) L, (7) J, (8) K, (9) A, (10) M, (11) N, (12) V, (13) S, (14) O, (15) T, (16) I, (17) E, (18) F, (19) B, (20) R, (21) Q, (22) U (23) W (24) X

Taken for a fool

(1) E, (2) Y, (3) C, (4) T, (5) A, (6) F, (7) B, (8) G, (9) R, (10) S, (11) H, (12) V, (13) I, (14) J, (15) K, (16) D, (17) M, (18) Q, (19) L, (20) O, (21) N, (22) W, (23) U, (24) P (25) Z (26) X

A date to remember

(1) F, (2) I, (3) H, (4) R, (5) S, (6) E, (7) D, (8) J, (9) M, (10) L, (11) O, (12) T, (13) G, (14) P, (15) U, (16) Q, (17) N, (18) C, (19) K, (20) A, (21) B (22) V

The one true thing

(1) F, (2) E, (3) C, (4) D, (5) G, (6) A, (7) J, (8) H, (9) B, (10) I

Bibliography

Fowler, H.W., *A Dictionary of Modern English Usage*, second edition, Oxford, 1978

Leech, Geoffrey, Benita Cruickshank and Roz Ivanic, *An A-Z of English Grammar & Usage*, Essex, 2014

Lloyd, Susan M., *Roget's Thesaurus of English Words and Phrases*, Essex, 1983

Partridge, Eric, *A Dictionary of Slang and Unconventional English*, Volume I, London, 1963

Partridge, Eric, *A Dictionary of Slang and Unconventional English*, Volume II, London, 1961

Room, Adrian, *Brewer's Dictionary of Phrase and Fable*, London, 2000

Shakespeare, William, *The Works of William Shakespeare*, London, Frederick Warne and Co.

Wood, Frederick T., *English Prepositional Idioms*, London, 1975

Wood, Frederick T., *English Verbal Idioms*, London, 1978

Printed in Great Britain
by Amazon